TH!

THE FIREMAN

A NOVELLA INSPIRED BY THE REAL-LIFE
ADVENTURES OF BENJAMIN WALKER

BENJAMIN WALKER B.A. (HONS) MIFIREE

Ignis Global Ltd

www.benwalkerfirefighter.com

ISBN 978-191241-922-7
Printed and bound in Great Britain.

Produced by YouCaxton Publications

Published by Ignis Global Ltd
www.benwalkerfirefighter.com

Disclaimer

This book is inspired by true events. Some of the characters, names, businesses, incidents and certain locations and events have been fictionalized for dramatic purposes. Any similarities to the name, character or history of any person is entirely coincidental and unintentional

Some of the names may have been changed, and some episodes and characters may have been blended and merged for the purposes of a better storytelling for you the reader. Some have wanted to remain anonymous, others in fear of reprisal.

So for record, let this story be regarded as a 'fictionalized account, inspired by real events & the reporting thereof'. But it remains up to you the reader, as to what you interpret and decide is true, what has been elaborated, what has been omitted because - only two people really know any one event at any one time.

What I will say though is, 'most of this shit actually happened'.

Foreword

Ben Walker is regarded today as one of the world's most influential fire service trainers and leaders. He has changed the way that firefighters are trained for the 21st century, through making the scientific easy to understand, from Burton on Trent to Buenos Aires; from Alaska to Australia.

However, this path was not taken through choice: from early promise and potential, Ben was forced into poverty, at one point becoming a professional pariah, untouchable and unwanted; even doing hard time in one of Britain's toughest prisons: for a crime he did not commit

So, forty nations and three books (to date) later, having altered the lives of firefighters and the communities they serve worldwide, this is his story. Some aspects have been altered to protect identities and those directly referenced have been done so with their permission. This is a shocking, brutal but ultimately uplifting memoir of the man known throughout the United States of America as the 'Firefighters' Cinderella Man'.

Not many could, or should have to walk his path, but the wise may learn from his mistakes. It's a measure of the man to bare his soul for the benefit of others: he doesn't ask to be recognized as hero, or victim; just a Man. We hope you learn and enjoy.

'Brother; God gives the largest crosses to bear, only to those with the broadest shoulders.'

Captain Andy Starnes,
Raleigh, NC to Benjamin Walker

The Code of the Firefighter:

Bravery Loyalty Courage Compassion

The four petals of the Maltese Cross. A code of honour for firefighters and a noble way for anyone to live their life. Aristotle, the Greek Philosopher said; '*Fame is the perfume of heroic deeds*'. Well, truly heroic deeds are underpinned by these four qualities.

I will be the first to admit that I am a deeply flawed individual; you will find this out as you read on.

I don't ask for sympathy or pity though; just an acknowledgement of what is right and what is wrong, I have a stubborn commitment to doing what is right. Some may describe me as brave, others as stupid, for exactly the same actions. But. I have always tried to live by this code of the firefighter. Sometimes it's got me into trouble, other times it's led to my downfall but in the end; I believe that the firefighter's code of trying to live our lives honourably, with integrity and humanity can save us all.

Benjamin Walker
March 2018

Contents

Chapter 1

Humble Beginnings

In my late twenties, I was a captain (UK equivalent) at one of the busiest firehouses (stations) in Europe. I'd served my apprenticeship in the unforgiving west, east and central areas of a northeast metropolitan fire department situated in Tyne & Wear and had made the hop over to the south side of the river and the Gateshead metropolitan district.

440,000 people, living in one of the most densely populated and poverty-stricken areas of the UK. One of the last remaining 'fire factories'.

My background has always influenced my approach to work and life. My parents were both from extremely poor backgrounds. Real poverty.

The Walkers, although descended from Roman-Celtic stock, were miners from south Nottinghamshire and northwest Leicestershire. Fighting, drinking and sports were about the only release from the drudgery of sixteen-hour shifts at the coalface. My grandfather died before I was born, when my father just twenty-one years old. My dad's mam, Nellie, was one of fourteen kids; the Ballards. Their father Ethelburt, was driven out of his native Black Country, after crossing swords with the 'Peaky Blinders' gang in Birmingham.

Mother's side of the family, at first glance appeared slightly more genteel. On the maternal side, they were churchgoing folk, relocated from the East End of London to South Derbyshire and the Rawdon/Cadley coal seam.

Appearances can conceal though; following the deaths of my grandparents, it was revealed that the initial move resulted from the union of an East End prostitute with a bigamous clergyman, who was on the run from both gangsters and the law. On the paternal side, the family's behavior was hardly angelic either. The theft, subsequent sale and disposal of a yellow diamond, obtained whilst 'in service' as a maid in British Colonial India, being another highlight.

So, my family background is piss-poor. Rogues, tinkers, thieves and fighters. However, certain things can be learnt from this. Ethelburt Ballard, who was chased out of the West Midlands by the Peaky Blinders, became known as 'Coalville's Memory Man', able to perform feats of recall and trivia in return for beer or money, to provide for his fourteen kids in a two-bedroom slum cottage. Walter 'Flower' Walker, Ethelburt's counterpart on the Walker side of the family, was a miner and a street fighter of some repute. Newspaper reports from 1901 report a bare-knuckle fight between him and the Irish Champion, taking place outside the Railway Tavern in Gelsmoor, northwest Leicestershire. Brains and brawn can both apparently pay dividends.

Education was at a premium in those days. My grandad Eric, was the youngest of four boys. Ralph the eldest, managed a grammar school education, as did the second son Reginald; whilst Joseph and Eric remained barely literate. My dad, whose parents Nellie and Eric, both with no formal education and barely literate, was firmly born into the cycle of poverty, growing up in 1950's and 60's rural mining communities.

Whilst at Newbold School, around the age of nine, a teacher noticed my dad's interest in nature and ability to draw (a talent that has not been passed down). Mr Stacey was a keen nature-lover and birdwatcher and he took my dad under his wing (excuse the pun) and worked hard with him to increase his education to a point where he could go on to take secondary education and obtain 'O-levels'.

With a God-given talent for sport and schoolboys' caps, playing for money by the age of seventeen, plus some hustle and bluff, my dad managed to break the cycle and lifted the Walkers out of poverty to a solidly working class level: to a point where there was always tea on the table.

Like so many who have climbed out of extreme poverty, my parents had an absolute commitment to hard work and a deep fear of returning to such conditions. I was brought up in an environment where the 'will to win', be it in life, education or sport, was everything. If an unpopular stance had to be taken to maintain integrity and 'win', then no apology was made. Life may have trodden on our families for generations but now, we were in a position to stand up for ourselves and confront our oppressors.

But who were they? Who are they?

Fighting, as I've said, is in my blood, physically and culturally. In an environment where underdogs were heroes, the escapism of cinema meant that Cool Hand Luke, Spartacus, Rocky Balboa and anyone who could beat the odds and the system, were revered.

I went to the local school in a very poor area but was encouraged and pushed all the time, both at home and by genuinely well-meaning teachers such as Mrs Wileman and Mr Chandler, who did their best to educate kids who had next to nothing. Our community had been devastated by the miners' strike, a couple of years earlier.

One of my earliest memories is playing football (soccer) in front of what seemed like a huge crowd: years later, I realized it was because so many of the other dads were out of work. Miners, in an industry decimated by the Thatcher government and let down by a union informed by its own political ambitions, rather than the welfare of its members.

It's funny how that theme came back into my own life some tweny-five years later.

I excelled at sport (rugby) and in education, so that in my teens, I won a prestigious full scholarship to a local independent school to sit 'A-levels' (high-school, senior/college-freshman equivalent). However, I suffered the misapplication of privilege, snobbery and abuse when it became known that my mother Nellie, was a cleaner for another pupil's wealthy family; with my fighting blood, this didn't end well and I was expelled, though still allowed to sit my 'A-level' exams.

In the end, I was fortunate enough to achieve excellent grades which allowed me to go to university and get a degree; entering the workforce and beginning my career in the fire service.

So, what did I learn from childhood and my upbringing? It's a question I've often asked myself.

It would be unfair of anyone and particularly myself, to critique my decisions as a child and teenager, with an outlook totally lacking in maturity. However, I do think that it instilled in me a sense of what's right, what's wrong and of the hard work needed to win. A sense of social injustice and a hatred of snobbery and inequality was engraved upon me. I also learned that life can be a series of chance meetings and to make the most of any opportunity, however oblique. Even, where necessary using some bluff, hustle and showmanship, whether sporting or intellectual, to achieve one's goals. But most of all; education or at least, the appearance of it, unlocks doors and overcomes hurdles.

Nobody gives it to you in this life. You have to take it!.

Jack Nicholson as Frank Costello,
The Departed, Scorsese 2006

Chapter 2

Milling Court Rescue

Which leads us to the point where I was in charge of the Gateshead Metropolitan fire station on a cold February night in 2010.

It was a bitterly cold northeastern evening, where spikes of cold cut like knives through the freezing air: we had just returned from a false alarm in the city centre, when the voice of the lovely Natalie in the control room came over our radio;

'Victor Zero One, Victor Zero Two, Charlie Zero One, Yankee Zero One, Yankee Zero Two, Whiskey Zero One, Victor Zero Three, Alpha Zero Seven... Proceed to flats on fire at Milling Court, Gateshead. Multiple persons reported in need of rescue. Several ambulances dispatched'

This was it; the big one. Whilst we were doing several fires a night, a big smoke alarm campaign of recent years had been a success. To the extent that mostly now, by the time we arrived, all persons were accounted for. The good-old or bad-old, days of smashing in doors and carrying people down ladders, which I'd had a final few years of as a young (handsome) firefighter, had for the most part, been consigned to history.

I knew I'd be on the spot as the first arriving Incident Commander. People and firefighters could live or die by the decisions that I made in a split- second, on the basis of what I could see and the information I could process.

There's a saying in the British Army; *'Proper prior preparation, prevents poor performances'* and this was certainly a mantra I adhered to. I was and remain, a perpetual student of firefighting. I'd recently read a book called '3D Firefighting' by Paul Grimwood, Ed Hartin, Shan Raffel and John McDonough (who I'm now privileged to call friends). The information it contained proved crucial on this occasion. I was always trying to innovate and refine approaches, sometimes to my own disadvantage.

The Tyne & Wear metropolitan area is a former heavy industrial area and very blue collar, where density of population is the largest hazard. Most properties are of 'terraced type' (US 'row-houses'), no more than two storeys high and two rooms deep, easy to ventilate externally and attack fires very rapidly. Short 'flowpaths'(air into the fire and smoke/fire/gas out to atmosphere) made a quick, aggressive approach very viable.

Having just had a recent verbal 'going over' from a Senior Divisional officer, for his belief that I was creating a system of 'predetermined assignments' (where firefighters automatically deploy to perform tasks rather than waiting for a full briefing), I was currently under suspicion of promoting an overly aggressive firefighting approach. Although not reckless, and probably spending more time on 'size up' and weighing up all risks-versus-benefits, I did try to implement the approach of '***Attack the Fire as a priority and all the other risks reduce accordingly***'. So, our first-arriving SCBA (self-contained breathing apparatus) crew would have the hoseline and be 'On the nozzle', performing what our American colleagues call 'Engine Company operations'. A fast knockdown of the fire was the aim. Big, bad and brash.

So; on the way to this incident, I was prepared: I knew the buildings and the layouts and I knew my firefighters were highly skilled and motivated operators, who could 'kick ass' swiftly...

Then something strange happened.

As we drove over the Tyne bridge and I looked at the city lights and the multi-coloured illumination on the Millenium 'Winking Eye' bridge, I was overcome with a sense of extreme calmness. I believe Buddhists call this a 'Zen-like' state. Whilst conscious of this happening, everything seemed to go into a kind of slow motion where I felt like I had all the time in the world. I was completely relaxed but heading to one of the potentially, most stressful jobs that any firefighter could encounter.

Arriving on the scene, I seemed to have a wider than usual perspective; as though my field of vision was twice its usual size. A scene of potential carnage was in front of me with flames and smoke billowing from the building, whilst people hung over first floor balconies, awaiting rescue.

Briefing one firefighter to make an initial knockdown with an external hose reel jet (transitional attack), the first crew made hose ready.

'Priority fire attack: hit it hard. It's already vented, so flood it. Don't worry about rescues until it's out. The next crews will get in and get them out'.

What happened next was like clockwork. Subsequent crews were briefed en-route and on arrival, jumped off their trucks and reported to entry control. They took a secondary hose reel and started emerging with people. Like pulling rabbits out of a magician's hat. Each firefighter in every crew was absolutely pin-point. They were superbly professional and completely motivated: looking back, they were really quite awe-inspiring

My messages to Control, included;

'Make Ambulances six. Correction seven, correction eight.... as the crews emerged with more and more people from the now steaming carcass of the building: signs that the firefighting crews had all but put this fire out.

During all of this, I felt a weird serenity: like conducting an Orchestra, with everyone playing in perfect synchronicity. A message over the handheld came from Jeff, the senior firefighter on our shift;

'It's all clear Ben. Fire's out. All persons accounted for. All areas checked by the BA crews'.

The transmission came loud and clear over my handheld and there was a collective sigh of relief from all other attending crews and officers. I spoke to the senior paramedic on the scene who confirmed that other than some minor burns and precautionary checks for smoke inhalation, we had collectively pulled out fourteen people. Fourteen 'grabs'. One of the largest fire rescues since the Second World War.

I verified some information and put the *'Stop &.All Persons Accounted.'* message into Control....

Whilst, the action may have been over, the most dangerous time at fire incidents can be when people visibly relax and lose concentration during overhaul or damping down. I've got a nice scar on my chest from a red-hot nail falling down my undone bunker gear some years ago. I gathered the multiple crews and briefed them to stay alert while we damped down to prepare the scene for Fire Investigators, I said something to them that I firmly believed at the time, although it embarrasses me a bit now.

'Well done gentlemen, you've just entered the pantheon of greatness in this brigade. No matter what else you do for the next thirty years, this will define your contribution. You are now legends.'

These were a group of younger guys who over the last two years, had replaced a very entrenched traditional shift at that station. They were an average age of maybe twenty-five or six and my words prompted a number of high-fives and fist-bumps. Maybe commonplace now but frightfully 'un-British' at the time. Both the Duty Divisional officer and Fire Investigator weren't at all impressed and called me to account for having an already dubious opinion of myself anyway,

'They're young. They're pumped up, high on adrenaline and they've saved over 10 fucking lives in the last ten minutes. How the fuck do you expect them to feel? This is what they joined the job to do!'

This was my response to the divisional officer,with whom I'd had some previous 'debate' over my 'aggressive' firefighting tactics. Perhaps not the wisest choice of words from an upstart officer, already under scrutiny for promotion of overly aggressive tactics and 'running a private fiefdom' from Gateshead Fire station.

How these words would come back to haunt me....

I know now that arrogance can be easily mistaken for conceit. As a younger man, I thought I was 'on top' of my game but when I look back, in retrospect I realize how little I actually knew. Within the parameters of one fire department and even one district, I felt I was King. I'd worked hard, put the time in and I felt some form of misplaced entitlement. What I didn't know was how inconsequential I was within the wider scheme of things even in the fire service, let alone ln the wider world of life.

Interpretation: how actions and words are perceived are important. It's part of the compassion and sensitivity element of the firefighter's code; the essential assets of the well-rounded officer or fire service leader.

Put interpretation and people's opinion, together with that arrogance and misplaced entitlement. I really didn't care what anyone else thought about me, bar my own satisfaction and the firefighters I was leading. How immature I really was at that time.

This is a difficult and subjective topic. Whilst we shouldn't live our lives worrying about opinions, personally or professionally; we also shouldn't ignore or steamroller them, as I did. A middle-ground must be struck between adherence to the righteousness of our 'mission', or life goals whilst still maintaining compassion and awareness. The skill is being able to differentiate: when to take notice of those worth listening to and when to ignore mindless critics. Finally, an old cliché. It's often said that pride comes before a fall: well, in my case, that was certainly true. The bigger the pride, the harder the fall.

We gathered around the mess table back at the fire station, celebrating with fish and chips and a special Caramac (candy) bar for Jeff's dessert. I sat in the middle of the long table watching the laughing and smiling faces, as the lads chatted, riffed and bantered with each other. It wasn't the last time I ate on shift with a crew, but this was certainly my 'Last Supper'. The only thing missing was a Judas Iscariot figure. Then, someone turned on the television.

When I saw the Divisional officer, Mick Walton, to whom I'd given my mouthful of industrial language, accepting the praise for our moment of glory on the regional news, the pride inside me spiraled out of control.

My mind was in full Cool Hand Luke, 'rebel without a clue' mode.

.If someone else is going to take credit for our hard work, well - fuck him - and fuck them.

An example and measure of my immaturity and emotional weakness at that time, which was to be very easily exploited...

Chapter 3

Losing

As the previous chapter implies I was, in some ways, 'out of control'. On the fire-ground, I was at peace; completely in control and almost 'zen-like'. Outside of that environment I was a bit of a mess, to say the least.

In my twenties, I'd been in a relationship with a school-teacher called Suzie: supportive, kind and an all-round good person. Both career-minded, we worked hard and progressed through promotions in our respective professions, whilst enjoying our social and home life. Good fun and mutual piss-taking; we were more like pals than lovers and I don't think she'd mind me saying that. A lovely person, who I only wish good things for.

We had rescued Barney, a big, white golden retriever as a one-year old, from a not very nice existence in Sheffield and we both doted on him. A regular fixture at the fire station, he was a gentle, loveable and docile beast and is pivotal to this story as well as being my best friend; or as the younger generation say now, BFF.

In late 2008, early 2009, Suzie called time on our relationship. There was no acrimony and nobody at fault; we were just moving in different directions. She wanted to settle down and start a family, whilst I was still (in my own mind anyway, though maybe not in that of others) on the upward trajectory that would inevitably end as Chief Fire Officer of the Tyne & Wear Metropolitan Fire Brigade.

I moved back to my own place in Jackson Street, North Shields; not far from the beach. It had been in a constant, casual occupation by a number of firefighters, getting divorced or separated and had been nicknamed 'the house of tears'. I quickly settled into the lifestyle of the single, 'upwardly mobile' professional.

I'd never been a drinker until now, being obsessed with my physical fitness and ability on the fire-ground. Now, Within walking distance of Tynemouth, a lovely coastal village with a number of pubs, bars, cafes and bistros, my days consisted of workouts and long walks on the shore with Barney.

The nights however, I spent alongside fellow firefighter John Butler, who'd joined the brigade and gone through the academy with me, with wine, women and song. Whilst neither of us would drink on a 'school night', both conscious of being sharp as a pin whilst on-duty, we certainly made up for it during these nights. It was once said, half-joking, that pretty well every woman in the greater northeast had either of our numbers in their phone.

Don't get me wrong, we had a great time. While the lifestyle we were leading at the time may not have been particularly pious or even admirable; we never lied, never hurt anyone and remained 'good' guys.

But, the bubble was going to burst...

Those of you who have read my factual reference books, may have noted the inscription at the beginning. *.Dedicated to the enduring memory of Paul Barrow and Billy Vinton..* Paul joined the brigade with Johnny Butler and me, changing in the same square metre of the dressing room, frantically rigging up whilst being screamed and bawled at by our instructors (all good people). A great guy, who'd done his time as a diver in the Royal Navy. Paul was everything we weren't, quiet and unassuming, getting on with things with minimal fuss. Solid. Good fun, with a very dry sense of humour. I thought a lot of Paul: the kind of guy who's the heart and soul of any fire station, engine or ladder company. A true professional.

Sadly, he was plagued by ill-health throughout his career; beating cancer twice within the first ten years of his career. Diagnosed for a third time, he finally succumbed to that horrible disease: may he rest in peace. One of my last memories of Paul is when Johnny Butler and I were taking the piss, trying to cheer him up with our gallows humour and Paul smiling and saying;

'At least you two can be relied upon to still be the sick bastards you are and I love you for it...

Billy was an 'old sweat'; a senior hand on the red watch at the old Newcastle east end Fosse Way station, in the busy areas of Walker, Byker and Heaton. Mickey Young and Bob Tiplady, two leading firefighters on the blue watch told me, after transferring in from the west end of Newcastle; *'We do things differently here.... We have local kids shipping the hydrants, we're undermanned and underpowered but we make it work.'*

Billy could always be relied upon to see the funny side of any situation that might arise during the handover from our dayshift to the red watch, coming on night duty and often had us in hysterics as the duty shift segued from days into nights. One of my greatest ever night-out drinking sessions was with Billy, following the annual soccer game the station used to play against colleagues from a southern England brigade. Life, love, loss, sport, politics and religion were all on the agenda as the drinks flowed. I always remember him telling me; *'Don't ever change. If you don't give them hell, nobody will!'*Billy also lost his battle with cancer shortly after his retirement. God rest his gentle soul.

So, where was I?

During this period, after losing two of the people I respected most, apart from my work and the dog, womanizing, drinking and living a rock-and-roll lifestyle were the only things that seemed to make sense. The only clarity I had was from clocking on duty, through to handing over to the next shift. No matter how crappy I was feeling, fires would always need putting out and people rescuing - and I was still good at that - surely things must get better?

Jake Gray lived next door to me in twenty-five Jackson Street. He was seventeen and from a loving single-parent family consisting of his mam Gill and brother Dan. Due to proximity, he became a sort of surrogate son or younger brother to me. I'd play basketball with him in his yard, drop him off at his mates and give him the 'benefit' of my own experience. He looked up to me as a sort of hero. When I moved back to North Shields, he became a real ally to me. When I was working our long fifteen-hour night-shifts, he'd stay at my place, take Barney for walks and watch DVDs some pals, or his girlfriend Paige.

I learned my lesson in some ways: I'm a big believer that alcohol shouldn't be a taboo subject for kids and told Jake if he wanted a beer, to help himself from the fridge. I even bought in a few standard lagers, Carling or Fosters for him. The next day though, these remained untouched, but my premium quality San Miguel had all gone. I had to laugh and appreciate that he certainly had good taste.

He was a fantastic kid.

The system for 'leave' in the Tyne & Wear brigade meant we could swap shifts with another office if we were unable to take regular leave. It was known as a 'knock-for-knock' but all 'paybacks' had to be made before January 31st of the following year. One day I got a call from Leslie Grantham, the station officer on white watch early in the New Year; *'I owe you a shift, and it's the last day I can pay you back, so I'll do tonight for you mate.'*

Now, I'd forgotten all about it and wouldn't have even noticed, so it was an unexpected bonus.

'Butler, get your threads on, we're out on the pull!'

Followed by my next phone call; *'Jakey, I'm off work tonight mate, so I don't need you to sit in with Barney.'* So, Jake was now at a loose end.

I remember that day well. It was a bitter, crisp morning and snow had settled on the beach; a rarity. Barney and I walked into Tynemouth, dropped down Priory Bay, round by Admiral Collingwood's Monument (The true hero of Trafalgar) and back along the Fish Quay. The weather began to turn and it became quite dismal and dingy.

One of Gill's many friends had a pal with a son who was studying at Leeds University, about ninety miles from Newcastle. Due to the snow, trains had been cancelled and Gill volunteered to drive this lad down to Leeds so he could get started on the new semester. Jake went along for the ride as he'd nothing to do that evening, now I'd dispensed with his services. A chain of events was set in place.

On the return journey, the A19 highway via Teesside was shut because of the snow, so Gill and Jake continued up the less familiar A1. As the weather worsened, they skidded and hit the central reservation in the blizzard-like conditions. Fortunately, they were OK and climbed out the car which was blocking the outside lane. They walked onto the hard shoulder to get assistance and rescue in the bitter night. While they waited there with the police en-route; an HGV, driving too quickly, swerved to miss the wreckage of their vehicle. Losing control, the wagon jackknifed and went off the road, dragging Gill underneath, causing horrific injuries and killing Jake instantly.

Our colleagues in County Durham Fire & Rescue service and Northeast Ambulance service managed to rescue Gill and get her to hospital and intensive care, where she was put in an induced coma. Jake was a body recovery. My friend Scott Forward in County Durham FRS, on discovering the connection, called me to offer condolences and assure me that their crews did all they could; which I never doubted.

Coming back from the pub, alone for a change, I saw a group of kids hanging around outside Jake's house. When I asked them what had happened, Paige burst into tears and Jake's friend Ross told me what he knew. In disbelief, I went into my own house and sat stunned, looking at Barney. Just a few hours ago, I'd told him I hadn't needed him to be here. If I'd been at work, then he would be here with Barney and not in a morgue in Darlington. If the snow hadn't shut the train lines - if the A19 had not been shut - if the weather had been better - if the HGV hadn't been speeding: was this fate at its worst? Were Paul and Billy taken from us for the same reasons? I took a huge slug on a bottle of Bourbon and passed out on the settee.

A few friends, Graeme Moore, Blaine Clancy and I, opened up our little gym collective for a charity day to raise money for Jake's funeral. Over 200 kids from the area turned up, taking over the sound system for freestyle dancing; they raised nearly £2000, which contributed to the cost of Jake's coffin.

The funeral arrived. Gill was in a wheelchair, only a day or two out of intensive care. Butler and I were there in our 'undress' uniforms, commemorating our young friend. As the coffin was interred at the crematorium in North Shields, the anthem 'My Brother Jake' by Free played over the tannoy system. As Paul Rodgers' gravelly vocals came over the airwaves, a single tear rolled down my cheek as we stood to attention. The words, although meant for Jake, felt like they were written to me;

'My Brother Jake, won't you start again?

Try making amends,

He goes out, he don't have no doubt,

He don't need to know, what the world's about.'

That night I opened a bottle of rum I'd been given by a firefighter from the British Virgin Islands. Usually, embarrassingly enough, I remember most of my awful antics of the night before but this was different: I remember nothing, from opening the bottle to waking up the next morning in bed with two young women - and Butler. I went to the bathroom and looked in the mirror full of self-loathing and disgust, overcome with shame and guilt.

Things needed to change.... I knew deep down, that I needed to start again.

The mind works in very different ways: it can be psychologically or physiologically affected by chemical imbalances such as excessive hormone release, or in other ways. I obviously had some kind of PTSD or traumatic disorder but I didn't understand this at the time and never fully appreciated that I needed some support. My ego, image and perception as a macho, rebellious, 'anti-hero' didn't allow me to admit speak about it, either to myself or to anyone else.

I really struggled alone, refusing to ask for any help which was stupid, as we had a brilliant brigade welfare officer, Linda (more about her later). I remember my former boss Joel Epstein, a London officer who'd moved to the north east, asking about my welfare. To my shame, I bluffed it out, turning it into some stupid confrontation when really, I felt like breaking down in tears.

I contacted him to apologise some months later and then again, some years later, while he was following his beloved West Ham. He accepted it without a moment's hesitation.

The irrational thoughts running through my head at this time began to take over, epitomized by the argument I had with Joel. Whenever I wasn't working, I obsessed about Jake, Paul and Billy, wondering if I was next: I almost convinced myself I too was going to die young.

I took a hard look at myself and thought the drinking, casual sex and revelry had to end. I needed to get a 'legacy'. If I was going to be dead soon then I urgently needed to do what mankind has always done for survival: procreate. I needed to settle down and start a family. Now. Emotionally vulnerable? ... Shockingly so!

Chapter 4

The Nightmare Begins

Emotionally vulnerable and with badly clouded judgment, I started looking for a mate. In hindsight, possibly the worst time to do this in my whole life. At the same time, I received an online message from a woman called Tamara; *'30 and looking for love'*. We arranged to meet on a Friday afternoon at the Metropolitan Bar on Grey Street in Newcastle city centre.

Sailors and fishermen around the North Shields Quays often talk about 'portents' and harbingers of doom. Understandably, in a river mouth where the infamous Black Middens rocks, hidden at high tides, have often shipwrecked heavily laden vessels, at the cost of many lives. Of course, I'd always dismissed this kind of thing as entertaining bullshit, while the craggy-faced old boys waxed lyrical in the Low Lights Tavern on the Brewhouse Bank. I half-expected them sometimes, to claim they'd seen mermaids or heard sirens singing.

In hindsight however, the analogy was very clear. Good navigation, taking heed of warnings, portents and gut feelings, sees a ship safely home. Too little caution or lack of concentration, can lead to shipwreck and disaster.

As I walked Barney around Admiral Collingwood's monument, overlooking the river mouth and the Black Middens that day, I looked out at the sky over the sea. It was purple - yellow - black - clear and heavy with thick clouds; all at once: Like a two-day old bruise. I can vividly recall it. I walked Barney home and as we turned into North King Street, the thunder and lightning began; mixed with snow. Bizarre.

The 'portents' were bad: The kind of afternoon that nobody in their right mind would set out on an adventure. Any captain with any sense would wait for this turbulence to pass before beginning his mission. Disturbed, lonely and grieving; I decided to set sail and navigate straight into the heart of the storm.

I met Tamara in the bar. The impression she created was that of a successful sales rep. from a multi-national family, with a successful business background. Having been a high achieving career woman, she too now wanted to settle down. Looking back, I think about 'cold reading', where a fortune-teller reads people's reactions and tells them the fortune they want. Tamara simply matched all the things I was saying. My stream of consciousness over mortality, legacy and all the fears brought on by losing my friends, was easy to match. The warning signs were obvious if only I'd looked - or listened.

While I sat in the bar waiting for her arrival, one of my favourite records began to play; 'Eminence Front' by The Who. All about appearances and façades. I'm sure that God or someone, was trying to warn me; it couldn't have been more obvious than if the bartender had handed me a copy of Oscar Wilde's 'Picture of Dorian Gray' with my change.

Where I perceived shared ambition and empathy, really it was surgical inquisition, exploring my insecurities and vulnerability. All for gain and advantage.

Sometime after, I found out via private investigations, that this Tamara was basically a highly manipulative woman, who extracted benefits, financial and otherwise from a succession of men, using threats and coercion. These included David McNeeley (A firefighter's brother- who incidentally, said nothing, whilst enjoying my disgrace), Grant Graham (A TV cameraman who'd worked on the Wire in the Blood detective series, Andrew Bowman... the list continues.... (*Names altered)

As we began seeing each other I did note odd aspects of her behavior, which under normal circumstances, might have rung alarm bells. I never met her family at any of their houses and never saw anything of her 'international import/ export firm'. I detected a fair amount of avarice and greed on occasions. I am a 'gentleman' of sorts and believe in chivalry: I open doors, pull out chairs and always offer to pay the bill at restaurants. However, it's nice if a partner occasionally offers to pay (whether accepted or otherwise). Tamara never offered and never paid for anything.

I never met any of her friends and when she talked about her former partner, it was highly derogatory; '*He was abusive to me, assaulting me, bruising me, threatening me.*'

She was quite compelling in her diatribe against this guy, holding eye contact whilst telling me; her poker face betraying no emotion whatsoever. I remember thinking at the time it was a bit strange; so matter-of-fact.

Even so, the overriding urge to settle and start a family prevailed. I was desperate and the fear of an early death that was driving me to create a legacy to prove that I existed, overcame my gut feelings or any sense of caution that things might not be quite right with her.

Very soon, she was dropping hints about getting engaged and like a fool, I was prodded into it. I won't say I went blindly but I was certainly wearing rose-tinted shades. I suppose in my heart, I hoped that once she had 'security', she'd begin to settle; things would balance out and the seas would calm. How wrong I was. I found myself bending over backwards for her, ignoring friends at her behest, apologizing for every little thing, even those I hadn't been responsible for.

At this time, I received a letter signed Davey Mc, stating that Tamara was a con-woman with a histrionic personality disorder and was a compulsive and dangerous liar. When I confronted her with it, she dismissed it as the words of a jealous ex, wanting her back. I accepted this and gave her the benefit of the doubt but I remember the physical gut feeling I got, that something wasn't right.

It turned out that Davey Mc's brother was a serving firefighter, working for a mentor of mine up in the west end of Newcastle but he neglected to mention his knowledge of this woman to anyone at all. Maybe he (and possibly others) wanted to see me brought down a peg or two; not realizing it would be a peg or ten!

Within weeks, she was pushing for a wedding and was insistent on a very small ceremony, with no guests. I found myself in front of Father Michael, at the Church of the Holy See in Jesmond, saying words which seemed to take an age to come out of my mouth. As if subconsciously, my body was trying to fight it. I can only describe it as like being drunk or in a dreamlike, schizophrenic state. Deep down, I knew something was wrong but I pushed on anyway...

She interrogated my text messages and after finding messages to Suzie (innocent enough - about the dog and the occasional night I couldn't get a dog-sitter), she produced a document that she claimed was an anti-adultery agreement. This, she said, was to give her peace of mind that she wouldn't be cheated on. To my own discredit, I signed the thing without even reading it.

We'll come to this later.

Fast-forward only a matter of weeks and my house in Jackson Street had been sold and another, forty-nine Southlands, was bought at auction. Tamara was insistent that she take charge of any renovations... requiring complete control.

I began to wake up from my daze. The first obvious cracks appeared: I began to notice that Barney, the world's best dog, would cower whenever she came near him. Leaving him with my family, I went to Enschede in Holland for a long weekend fitness conference with a young man who'd been invited into our fitness collective.

On my return, when I went to withdraw some cash for a taxi back from Newcastle Airport and was confounded to see 'Insufficient Funds' on the screen. I knew that, given my house sale equity, I had a substantial amount of money in this account but where had it gone to? Taking the 'Quick Statement' option, I tried to find out what had happened to the money...

She had shifted my money to her own control!

I remember riding on the Metro back from the airport to West Jesmond, then cutting through the Dene and up to Southlands. I felt, conversely, as if a huge weight had been lifted off my shoulders: as if a blindfold had been removed.

To quote Samuel L Jackson in Pulp Fiction; *'I experienced what alcoholics refer to as a moment of clarity.'* At that moment, I knew this was bad and that I should not be in this situation; with this woman.

Opening the door, I demanded of her;

'What the fuck is going on with my money?'

'Well, I'm the one in control of this relationship, so I should have the money and you should do what I say.' 'Look, this is a huge mistake. Honestly, I do think this has been a big, big mistake. I'm going to go away for a few days. I don't want to be here, or to be with you. Let's both walk away and chalk it up to experience. I've not been myself for ages but I can see now how I've lost my way.'

I took some leave from work and took the dog to my parents' little smallholding down in the West Midlands, before arranging to meet her at our marital home on the 6th October, to sort things out once and for all. I knew I'd be subject to a horrendous amount of piss-taking at work, and could also lose a lot of money but I decided to regard it as all part of life's rich tapestry. I was in a position where I could quite easily write the experience off; like John Lennon's 'Lost Weekend' and get back onto my trajectory that would still, inevitably; end with me becoming Chief Fire Officer!

I engaged a solicitor and started divorce proceedings by gaining a separation order and freezing our assets, to make sure that the £40k didn't rapidly disappear. This was sent to Tamara, notifying her in advance of my return. The solicitor told me; *'Don't worry, due to the short term of the marriage, it is usual that both parties take back what they put in and go their separate ways. The only exception is if one party has given up work or has been under duress.'*

I'm a believer that all mammals have a latent sixth sense. A cat anticipates things and acts before he can possibly see; often cheating death. Hence, the nine lives of the feline. Humans may have lost this overtly but at times, a gut feeling or hunch pays dividends: Columbo solving a crime, the soccer manager taking a chance on an unlikely hero... gut feelings should be listened to. If a gut feeling tells you something is wrong... It probably is.

Chapter 5

First Arrest

So, we arrive at the 6th October.

Trying to develop an equitable exit strategy, I felt that to extricate myself from the situation, we should both take out what we had 'brought to the table' and that £10k compensation to her, would be a reasonable, even generous solution. I thought that, yes, we've fucked up here, so let's get back to how we were before we met. I knew I would lose some money but thought that if I ensured she had not lost anything, then that should compensate for any public embarrassment.

How wrong I was.

When I opened the door at number forty-nine, I was met by a whirlwind of vicious aggression from her: screaming and shouting at me and waving a piece of paper.

I told her what I thought and then she hit me with a bombshell; *'I'm going to take everything from you. You can walk away now with nothing and sign everything over to me, or I'll take your money, your career and your life... and if I see your bastard dog, I'll stab it through the neck!'*

While her words spewed like bile, I noticed she was looking at her (expensive) watch: it was coming up to 10am...

'You just better fuck off! I want you out this house by the end of this week, with all your shit and I'll see you in court, you evil cunt!' Not my most eloquent or erudite response.

I strode to the front door and was just about to open it when she flung herself to the floor next to me. When I opened the door, two police officers were standing there in front of me. They looked at me and then at her, lying on the floor and clutching her head. They read me the rights....

'We are arresting you on suspicion of domestic assault. You do not have to say anything, but if you do not say anything it may impact on your defence in a court of law....'

'Is this a fucking joke?'

By the time we got to Market Street police station, next to the old Pilgrim Street fire station, I was raging with indignation and injustice. I was handcuffed and marched down the old Victorian corridors to the cells. I was stopped at a corner, where two coppers both hit me in the face: one with a fist, the other with a forearm; before pushing me to the floor... *'Oh look - he's tripped over... he seems ok though - I'll fill in the accident report.'* I'm savvy enough to know that this was a 'blind spot' on the CCTV, so what would be the point in reporting it - eh?

Slung in the cells, I found out for the first time that British law allows a suspect to be held without charge for up to twenty-four hours. Could it have been possible that Northumbria police liked to hold a suspect for as long as possible to 'soften them up' prior to interviewing them?

After being stripped and my soaking clothing removed, I was marched to an interview room eight hours after my arrest. With only a police blanket wrapped around me like a toga, I met the duty solicitor (US public defender) Steve Davies, who reminded me of the British actor, Jimmy Nail. I sat down for my first ever police interview as a suspect.

Explaining the circumstances, I challenged the statement of the arresting officers. The female officer claimed that, as she approached the property, she could see Tamara cowering next to me as I verbally berated her, which constituted the offence of 'Common Assault'.

I pointed out that the door was solid wood with no vision panels and Mr Davies immediately accused the police officer of attempting to pervert the course of justice. The interview was terminated. As I shook his hand and prepared to leave, I looked at the female officer and said;

'There's only one thing worse than Cops.... Bent Cops.'

During the interview, I had asked why they had turned up; *'We received a call from Tamara's mother, saying she was in fear of you and that you were smashing the house up and threatening her with a power drill..'* The image of her checking her watch flashed through my mind: Had they conspired to set me up? Bitches.

Fully expecting to be released; I stood up to go, only to be immediately re-arrested for 'Making threats to kill' and slung back in the cells. Following further protests from Steve, I was 'de-arrested' then 're-arrested' again; this time for public disorder. After the twenty-four hours was up, I was finally released.

Collecting my kit from the new desk sergeant, he spoke quietly to me; *'I hear you're a friend of Barry McSheedy's (another firefighter). Mind how you go and make sure you're covered. I've seen too many blokes here getting stitched up by scorned women.'*

I walked up Northumberland Street. In Newcastle and Blacks (an outdoor store which was having a sale), I bought two North Face coats for £120, which I still wear.... Maybe this was a metaphor for the cold winters to follow. Rod Stewart's unplugged version of 'Mandolin Wind' played over the radio; *'The Coldest Winter, in almost fourteen years, could never change your mind.'*

Chapter 6

The Campaign Trail (of hatred)

As I turned up for duty, one of the young guys came up to me and said; *'The D.O's here; wants to see you in his office.'* As I passed through the canteen upstairs, Butler shouted over to me, lifting a mug of tea to his lip sand revealing the base that had been printed with *'I AM A TWAT'* he smiled and said; *'I hope Walton doesn't mind me drinking from his cup!'*

I opened the door, expecting Walton, the same guy who'd given me the shaft at Milling Court and thinking that a confrontation would ensue about his TV appearance accepting the plaudits: instead there was a friendly, familiar face sitting behind the desk.

Shane McQueen was a former Royal Navy field gun crew member, Combined Services boxing champion, England gymnast and an all-round awesome guy. He and I were kindred spirits; I'd followed Shane up the ranks, having about five years less service time than him and he'd been my boss on a number of occasions. We were well known for sharing the same absolute dedication and will to win at operational incidents.

'What's happening wor kid? Word is you're getting some shite from a crazy cow!'

'Well, you know that Shane, or you wouldn't be here -.what's the crack?'

'Well mate, you won't believe this, but she's started making allegations against everyone – left, right and centre - so 'Churchers' (CFO Brian Churchgate) is pulling you off.'

'Isn't he going to buy me a drink first?'

Thus ended my operational time in the Tyne & Wear Metropolitan Fire Brigade. I was shifted to the training school, working for my old training officer Vic, and placed 'off radar'- temporarily at least.

It transpired that Tamara had made several complaints to the brigade and to the police (not knowing I was off duty), alleging that she had been rammed off the road by fire trucks: an allegation quickly disproved by revealing to everyone's surprise, including many bewildered firefighters, that our appliances had GPS trackers fitted to them.

Another highlight was a letter to the Fire Minister's office, after these complaints had been rejected by the chief and the fire authority chair, claiming that the brigade was being run to carry out a personal vendetta against her, at the behest of myself and the chief fire officer.

Perhaps the final straw for me was her allegation against S; a very good friend and a superb firefighter but with a lively temperament and a noted short fuse. She claimed he had assaulted her in a Newcastle Bar and the Northumbria police arrested him as he was due to leave home to collect his son. As his wife was working away and without phone reception, his five-year old son was stranded at school, while he suffered the same indignities as I had: being locked up for twenty-three hours before being interviewed and showing he was actually on duty, having swapped a shift on the night in question.

He never blamed me but I couldn't help feeling responsible for that little boy's distress.

She was fighting a campaign against me. By proxy if necessary - with increasingly outrageous claims - Surely nobody would take her seriously? Except detective constable (DC) Kelly Darkman, that is.

A detective in the police force leaked some information, sitting in his car at the back of West Denton fire station one night, telling me that DC Darkman was noted in his hatred for Firefighters, rumours in the police were that he had been married to one. I was told that he had also been subject to internal disciplinary proceedings for sexism and 'inappropriate relationships with victims'. A match made in hell, teaming up with Tamara.

About four weeks after my initial arrest the campaign kicked into overdrive. Darkman arrested me on several occasions, in response to historic allegations made against me by Tamara, none of which had been reported when they allegedly happened, several months earlier. I was quite polite initially but after the arrest for 'sexual assault', I asked DC Darkman if he was a moron.

I was held for what seemed like twenty-three hours until I was interviewed and a statement made by Tamara, was read out, which had prompted the arrest for sexual assault; '*He came in from work in a foul mood, swept me off my feet and slung me over his shoulder. He carried me upstairs and threw me on the bed. In one swift motion, he ripped my knickers off and laughed, saying; 'I'll be having a slice of that, my dear!'*'

Danielle Jackson, who had become my solicitor, representative and top of my speed-dial, burst out laughing and as soon as the 'tape' was stopped said; '*Well that sounds like a pretty good night from my perspective!... Are we done here or do you want to persist with the Mills & Boon bollocks?*'

So, it went on; arrest - release, arrest - release... I began to taunt DC Darkman out of frustration and she made it personal, remarking to two firefighters Jim & Graeme, who crossed paths with him; *'I'm going to get that bastard and I don't care if he's done it or not!'*

Looking in the mirror at my tired face, I noted a white spot on my face and running my fingers through my hair, clumps of hair came out. This was all I needed... alopecia. Well - I was never going to be as suave as Connery in James Bond, but at least I'd be bald like him!

Surely this couldn't carry on?

It was a Monday morning at the brigade training centre, recently supplanted to the new Headquarters building, the nerve centre of this major metropolitan fire brigade. Over 400 staff, uniforms, civilians, recruits, instructors, and managers, all in a huge open-plan premises, with eyes and ears open.

Preferring more privacy, I was working in one of the small meeting rooms on the training school side of the buildings and was reviewing some ventilation procedures for Victor, an instructor who'd trained me as a recruit many years before, when there was a knock on the door. An ashen-faced young civilian staff member stood beside a smirking Darkman and two of the biggest coppers that the force could muster.

'I've fucking got you now!' He sneered, as I was banged face-down onto the desk. My arms were wrenched up my back and handcuffs, solidly connected with a bar, snapped on. At this point Kevin, a kindly senior officer showed up and shouted; *'I don't think there's any need for that!'*

Darkman responded in the most industrial language, that he too would be arrested if he interfered.

Rather than take me down the stairs and through the old training school reception, Darkman took the decision to parade me through the training school itself, across the upper walkway in the wrong direction, past the main open plan office and all the HQ staff. This posturing and display of superiority filled me with hate but the only thing running through my mind was; Don't look intimidated. Laugh at them and pretend you're Steve McQueen in the Great Escape, being marched to the cooler by two Nazi goons.

After the usual many hours in custody, I was interviewed again: referring back to my first arrest, it transpired that two new witnesses, Tamara's mother and her friend Davis Peters, had come forward to verify her claims. Why were these alleged witnesses not mentioned at the time, or in any prior interviews/allegations? Because they weren't there, that's why.

Danielle made angry representations to this effect, stating it was more than coincidental that this hadn't been mentioned at the time - and now two witnesses had appeared out of thin air, just before the statute of limitations was reached...

Back in the cells, a smirking Darkman came in with a piece of paper, stating that despite a complete absence of any physical evidence, any reports at the time, or the fact that it was all a construct in the mind of a demented woman, her co-conspirators and a Fireman hating detective being all-too willing to shaft a cocky fireman, the Crown Prosecution Service deemed that two 'independent' witness statements, along with that of the (discredited) original arresting officer with the X-Ray vision) sufficed to pass the 'threshold test' and was sufficient to charge me with the crime of 'Common Assault..

The next morning, I was taken to Newcastle magistrates Court to enter a plea.

'Not Guilty'.

The Lady Magistrate looked over at me and set a date for a late January trial in magistrates Court. At that point, Darkman asked to make a statement and the CPS lawyer invited his comment;

'Due to the serious fear in which the alleged victim now lives due to this man and to the potential for witness intimidation, Northumbria Police and the CPS strongly recommend that this man should be remanded in custody until trial.'

Looking at the alopecia-ridden, shaven-headed, broad-shouldered, tired-looking firefighter standing opposite, the Lady Magistrate declared icily; *'To be remanded in Her Majesty's Prison Durham, until trial.'*

What the Fuck? I was going to jail - for something I hadn't done!

Prison transport vans consist of a number of cubicles about the size of a shower tray: these contain a resin seat and a door with an aperture so you can push your handcuffed wrists through to be released whilst in transit and re-cuffed before arrival. There is a small semi-frosted window but enough to see out of when standing up. A number of other men were lined up and handcuffed as we were led on by the security guards responsible for this transport. The radio in the van played and was piped through into the cubicles. I was positioned in the rear right-hand side of the van.

We pulled out of the magistrates court yard to the Crown Court on Newcastle's quayside and the process was repeated. I heard some commotion and cursing, as possibly three more were led on for their sponsored taxi ride to jail.

'Here comes the Rain' by the Eurythmics played over the stereo as the van proceeded down the A167, through the houses and cottages of Low Fell and Gateshead. I looked out of the small window. Only a matter of weeks before, I had 'owned' these streets; responsible for the safety of the 440,000 persons in that district. Now, I wasn't sure what was going to happen. I was alone; without any idea of what lay ahead.

We passed Anthony Gormley's behemoth sculpture, 'The Angel of the North'; her arms spread wide in a symbol of welcome and hope. I was pretty sure that hope had almost gone; there were no angels watching over me now. I tried to keep my eyes on the sculpture until the angle of the window narrowed and it fell away out of view.

The DJ came across the speaker; *'That was the Eurythmics. Now this is Jermaine Stewart with – 'We don't have to take our clothes off to have a good time'.* A voice shouted out; *'I hope the big men on the (prison block) wing feel the same way!'*

I laughed - well - what else could I do?

Chapter 7

Welcome to E-Wing-
Durham Prison Blues

We pulled into Old Elvet, in the ancient city of Durham, with its magnificent cathedral overlooking the spur in the river Wear. Under normal circumstances this place was a pleasure to visit. This was somewhat different.

We were marched, handcuffed in single file into the wing for processing. I thought of training school and told myself I'd better get my head back in that mode. I won't refer to the prison guards as 'screws': I always speak as I find. A couple of the guards looked at my uniform and one said;

'What are you here for?'

'Remand, Sir. I replied; *'Which Offence?' 'Common Assault.'*

'You don't get remand for that, it's not even a custodial offence.' 'Apparently I do Sir.'

He flipped through his clipboard and found my paperwork. With a look of surprise on his face he walked over to me and said; *'You shouldn't be here but seeing as you are, I will tell you this. Keep your head down, don't make enemies, call the guards boss, not Sir and I'll keep an eye out for you.''Yes, boss.'*

Moving through the processing in jail, I had to remove my work boots (steel-capped) and fire brigade uniform. I was handed a set of grey sweatpants and crew neck sweatshirt, told to remain naked and proceed to one of three cubicles and stand directly above the mirror. *'Spread your arse cheeks and squat down over the mirror, prisoner.'*

The check for 'plugged' contraband had begun. Initially, I felt my dignity was being assaulted but as I was told to stand up and turn around to have my penis and testicles examined (apparently genital and anal warts are rife in British prisons), I made eye contact with the guard and I could see he was just trying to do his job. He didn't enjoy the experience any more than the prisoners did but like so many hours spent mopping firehouse floors as a probationary firefighter, it was a necessary part of the job.

We were given a verbal briefing by the lead officer on E-Wing before being taken to the exercise yard. It was a bitterly cold day but the sun shone brilliantly in an ice-blue sky. I tucked into a sheltered spot and lifted my face towards the sun, feeling a brief ray of heat on my face before hearing; *'Time's up. Back in.'*

While the cells were being designated for the new arrivals, a number of prisoners came by for 'association', a brief reprieve from being inside the cell. I saw two lads from North Shields, Des and Dave who used to train at the old YMCA gym. As they passed, Des said to me; *'What the fuck are you doing here?'*

People and their values are strange and fleeting things: as I stood in line, I saw Des speaking with one of the guards and overheard him; *'He's not meant to be here boss. That guy is a fireman, a proper hero; he's not one of us. I mean, he's sound, not a grass or anything but he's a straight player. He's not a criminal.'*

I never knew Des very well, other than giving him an occasional 'spot' whilst lifting in the gym. I haven't seen him since then and I don't know where he is now but I sometimes wonder why he felt compelled, on that cold winter day, in one of Britain's oldest and toughest jails, to speak out on behalf of someone he didn't really know.

My first night in jail, I was 'padded up' with an old boy with a crazy beard, spectacles and terrible halitosis. Feeling something sharp as I went to get into the bed, I felt a razor blade. Fortunately, I'd only touched the flat edge and not cut myself. For the rest of the night, I listened to the occasional shouts, insults and quiet sobbing of others doing 'time' at what the Brits quaintly call; 'Her Majesty's Pleasure'.

'Walker, get up!' A guard opened the cell at 5.45 the next morning. *'You've got a new job -wing cleaners.'* Wing cleaners are basically prison orderlies, who can be trusted to act responsibly and are allowed out of the cells in working hours: performing such menial tasks as mopping floors, painting railings and balustrades and giving haircuts with a set of safety clippers.

I was issued a set of green pants and shifted to a cell with a Middlesbrough native, Lee: a smuggler by trade, who described his stretch as an occupational hazard and accepted doing the time. Mentally, this was a lot like being back at training school. That extra freedom of not being in the cell was a real bonus to me. I threw myself into it and did all I was asked. Wing cleaners also got the opportunity to use the gym at 6.00hrs, so I began training; hard and heavy.

I'm thirteen-and-a-half stone, 5'10. with the build of a Staffordshire bull-terrier, so I was never an obvious target for any prison beatings but I remained alert for trouble. A few threats had been thrown around between criminal families from Newcastle and Sunderland and trouble was brewing on the wing...

One of the wing cleaners' duties was to serve the food at meal times. Made in a central kitchen, huge containers were bought onto the wing, containing the various culinary delights that prisoners working on their catering skills, had created. Prisoners would queue up, grab a tray to receive their food and then return to the cell to eat, before being locked in again for the afternoon stint. The usual arrangement would be meat of some description, some mash, a vegetable and a slice of bread, followed up if lucky, by gravy. Those dishing out the grub usually assumed set positions. My role was mop man; standing at the end of the delivery, ready to deal with any spillages or debris caused by the rapid feeding of a wing-full of prisoners.

The food came in chaperoned by the central prison orderlies who were randomly selected every day and the food each wing received was unknown, due to some prior tampering with food being prepared for prisoners in protective custody, such as high-profile murderers or paedophiles. Everyone got into position and the long snaking queue collected their trays.

As usual, grey-coloured meat was slapped onto trays, potatoes dumped, veg dropped and gravy slathered... A few cursory sweeps of the mop and things were looking good. Suddenly however, the queue halted; one of the prisoners hadn't moved on but just stood, eyeballing the 'gravy man'. A full mouthful of vile spit, saliva and sputum came over the trestle table, swiftly responded to by a ladle of red-hot gravy: trays were dropped and tables overturned and then I saw it.

Out of the corner of my eye, a shiv was swung like a left hook, towards Gravy's head. As a complete reflex, I caught the attacker's inside left wrist about four inches from Gravy's eye.

'What the fuck ah ye deein?' were the last words as two burly guards took him down to the floor in a restraint. *'Ye're fuckin dead ye – dead!'* he screamed as he was dragged away.

What had I got myself into now? I couldn't stand by and watch someone killed or permanently crippled, but was I now going to be a target? Getting interviewed in the aftermath, I stuck to the line that I was merely mopping up the spilt food and hadn't seen or been involved in anything.

'Very wise, son.' a seasoned officer remarked as I was chaperoned back to my cell after interview. The mood on the Wing was toxic; some form of revenge attack had been foiled and blood was wanted... Not happy times.

One of the advantages as a wing cleaner was the large television on the landing by our cells. Depending on which duty guard was on, MTV or VH1 was allowed to blast out; a welcome relief while polishing bannisters with a tin of Brasso for the umpteenth time. On the evening following the lunch table rumble, an 80's collection was playing on the TV and suddenly, Freddy Mercury and Queen burst forth from the speakers: 'Radio Ga-Ga', playing at top volume.

Just for a bit of devilment, I started banging on the cell door in time to the handclaps as was famously seen at Live Aid in 1985. Within a few beats, the whole landing joined in and then the entire wing. Completely surreal; all these hardened prisoners in one of Britain's toughest jails, clapping along to the command of one of the greatest but campest rock performers of all time.

I was told later that even the guards found this highly amusing and I was woken with a smile next day by the officer who'd conducted my intimate search; *'Walker, you're out. Trial's been delayed. Your brief has seen the judge in chambers and you've been bailed.'*

As I collected my belongings in a clear plastic bag, I went through the processing and thanked the guards, looking each in the eye; *'In the nicest possible way, I hope I never see you again!'*

'Mind how you go, eh?'

And with that, I was standing in front of the Archetypal Prison Gate as the roller shutter went up.

Not knowing what I would find, I saw Butler, in tears; *'I've been sent to get you away mate.'*

So, where to now?

Chapter 8

Tyneside to Trentside.

'*Mate... I'm so sorry.*' Butler handed me an envelope with my name, rank and number on it. I opened it up; 'You have been suspended on full pay until conclusion of your criminal trial, scheduled for 7th and 8th of April. Please feel free to remain in contact with your Liaison Link, Senior Divisional officer McQueen and brigade welfare officer, Linda Lauren. We remain committed to supporting you through this difficult time'. Signed by the C.F.O, Brian Churchgate.

I understood he was doing the right thing and to quote a cliché, getting me 'Out of Dodge' but it was a huge wrench that my work was being taken away.

It was a few days before Christmas and I felt completely empty as we stood on the frosty ground in the shadow of the Victorian prison gates,. What is a man without purpose? What does the warrior do in peacetime?

We embraced: two old friends. We'd trained together, fought fires together, drank together, done everything.

'The Boss wants you down at your mam and dad's. The Deputy's going to speak to Notts and Derby Brigades, see if they can have you 'on loan'.'

'Well, in that case mate, I better be going.'

Butler drove me to the train station and waited with me for the cross-country train to Plymouth, calling at each station in between. My items had been returned in a plastic bag when leaving the jail and I sat on the train, back in uniform, staring out the window. I plugged my iPod in, set to shuffle: the opening bars of 'Long, Long, Way from Home' by Foreigner, blasted through the earphones. The irony wasn't lost on me: although I was returning to the place of my youth, I couldn't have felt more far away.

The phone rang while I was between York and Leeds. Kenny Davidson an old friend, fondly referred to as DCI Gene Hunt, after the Life on Mars character was on the other end; *'Right mate, you've not heard this from me kid...'*

Apparently following my arrest and prior to being charged, a meeting had been convened with representatives from a number of bodies. Tamara had claimed that she was pregnant (by me), which is an 'aggravating factor' in UK law and can influence decisions to charge accused persons.

She didn't know though, that the Chief Superintendent of Newcastle's brother Greg, was a legislative fire safety officer, who had worked with me before. I assume something was said.... Sitting around a huge table at the Etal Lane police station, were the Chief Superintendent, DC Darkman, social services, child protection and the fire brigade's welfare officer, Linda.

Now, my friend Shane was out commanding an incident; so my nemesis Mike Walton, had stepped in.

'I've heard this guy Walker is meant to be pretty sound.' said the Chief Superintendent; *'So, is this a case of a scorned wife slinging as much mud as she can at everyone? I've heard she's complaining to every man and his dog.'*

'Well, to be honest sir, he's definitely a loose cannon and in my personal opinion, I wouldn't put it past him...' Walton piped up uninvited.

I was told later that Linda's jaw almost hit the table: the sheer shock soon replaced by embarrassment and anger. A man's future was at stake and an objectionable climber, scared of fighting fire for real, chose that moment to try and remove some competition for his next promotion!

Back to the phone call with the Kenny Davidson; *'Say nothing Ben, talk to me and me only from work. Understand?'*

'Of course.'

'Good lad. Keep ahowled and I'll see you soon.'

Burton Upon Trent is a strange town.

Once the epicenter of beer brewing, exporting ales throughout the British Empire, like other traditional industries, it has seen a decline. The town is now propped up by huge logistics operations and massive warehouses, attracted by its central position, straddling the east and west Midlands with easy access to the M1 & M6, Birmingham and Nottingham Airports.

A mass immigration of cheap foreign labour in the early 2000's has seen an influx of eastern Europeans alongside the Asian and Afro-Caribbean communities, established here since the 1960s. There's an uneasy truce between these groups, so that the streets I played in as a child, are now dominated by gun and knife crime, terrorism and recent modern slavery arrests.

In contrast, there are some very good takeaways. Not many places outside of London where you can get a Turkish coffee, Kurdish kebab, Greek baklava, Bangladeshi biriyani, Jamaican jerk chicken and Polish sausage all within a few doors.

As I got off the train, plastic bag in hand; the fragrance of hops filled my nostrils. I flashed back to my childhood, playing rugby on the Ox Hay meadows where the river Trent splits in two. Breathing in the smell, I thought I might as well have a pint. I walked up station Street and turned right onto the high street, passing the banks and the market place. My iPod played in my ears; 'Bad Company' by Bad Company; 'Behind a gun, I'll make my final stand.'

I had no gun, but I had to make a stand.

The Leopard is a London-style pub on Lichfield Street, with the market place and the Abbey on one side and the rugby club on the other. I walked along like so many times in my teens and opened the door.

'Fuck me! Am I seeing a Ghost?'

'Alright Paul?'

Paul Insley had been my friend since childhood. Ten years older than me, Paul had unwisely volunteered to step in and coach the Burton under-eights junior rugby team over twenty years before and got the bug, becoming coach, mentor and friend until seeing me off at eighteen into the big wide world. He'd taken over as landlord of the Leopard with his wife Elaine. His brother Andy, having just returned from selling his seaside bars in Spain, also sat with us, along with Rob, another old friend.

'I take it you'll be having a drink then?'

'You take it right.'

Paul poured the drinks and we moved round to sit in the snug; *'You've not still got that old thing up have you?'*

I looked at the wall: a framed Rugby shirt with an action photo of myself at nineteen, ball in hand, hung behind where Paul was sitting; *'Well, that guy was my star pupil. Would've played for England in the World Cup Final if he'd kept his fucking mouth shut!'*

We drank into the night, Andy regaling us with tales of Spanish adventures, reminiscing about old times. Gradually, my current predicament came out. I told them that although I was innocent, I felt I was playing against a rigged deck: the incessant allegations and constant arrests.

'Look at that guy on the wall.' Paul said; *'I've never seen anyone play with such will to win and refusal to give up. Remember us playing versus the East Midlands under floodlights when you were seventeen? We were getting hammered but still in touch and I switched you to play out of position at scrum half to get you on the ball more. What happened?'*

I remembered the game. We were outmanned and outclassed but we remained in touching distance. With twenty minutes to go, we had a huddle and looked in each others' eyes. What happened next was that our bunch of ragtag local lads outfought, out-scrapped and beat a regional side consisting of four future England internationals. They were better players but in those circumstances, our collective aim, our self-belief, friendship and will to win had prevailed.

'You've got to fight this through; never give up. And the worse things seem, the harder you have to fight. Because I know you'll win. You don't know how to lose.'

I slept that night at the pub and in the morning, I walked up the Branston Road in the darkness; back to my parents' smallholding farm on the edge of town.

I dreaded walking in and tried to think of something clever or funny to say, to no avail. The best I could muster was; *'Dear Mother... Sell the pig - I'm coming home!'*

My mother sat there crying but my dad, stoic and pragmatic, was looking for a solution, not the problem. As I sat with my him and explained the circumstances, he asked me what the crack was with lawyers. We picked through the allegations and worked out there were several inconsistencies in each of the statements made by the opposition. Things that didn't add up or corroborate, coupled with the fact that these were 'historical'; not made when they were alleged to have happened. Danielle Jackson had told me that as soon as a judge looked at them, he would dismiss the case against me and probably severely reprimand Northumbria police and the CPS.

'Look, I've got a bit of savings put aside. Do you think we should get a shit-hot Queen's Counsel up from London to get this put to bed?'

My dad put to Danielle on a conference call that afternoon; *'I don't think that'll be necessary. I've got a wonderful lady barrister who's an expert in this type of thing.*

Her in Newcastle and local judges don't like Cockneys coming up here.' replied Danielle.

We went with her judgment: I still believe that Danielle was extremely well meaning but her choice of barrister was a mistake that would have far reaching consequences.

In this interim period, Tamara contacted me via phone and during a bizarre call, threatened me but also offered an inducement, to hand over all my money and she would drop charges. I reported this offically to Staffordshire police: a PC Holding took my statement, with the relevant reference number 692. To be fair to Staffordshire police, I believe that they would have passed this information to the investigating officer in Northumbria, Darkman, but would any action ever be taken to stop this badly acted farce?

So, we were preparing for trial: Barney was settling in at my parents and Christmas was upon us. By this time, I was completely bald through the alopecia, with de-pigmented skin all over my head and face; just in time to be knocked for six by pneumonia and swine flu.

Delirious with fever, I kept imagining I was sitting at the fire station table with my dead friends, Billy, Paul and Jake, all laughing and joking; then looking at me saying; '*You must never give in Benny Boy. Never!*'

I came out of the illness around the 7th of January. Christmas and New Year were just a blur. I stood on the scale and looked at my weight: eleven stone, ten pounds. I was nearly two stones lighter than I should be. I had to get healthy and quick.

Over the next few months, I followed a regimented routine: get out of bed and take Barney for a long walk, then head to the gym and train. After that, I'd go to the library for an hour's reading on criminal law, followed by at least two hours of fire-related material. Some pivotal material was digested, dissected and processed. '3D Firefighting', Brunacini's 'Command Safety', Norman's 'Officers' Handbook', Grimwood's 'Eurofirefighter' and 'Fog Attack'. I was determined to stay on top of my game, ready at any moment to get back into the saddle.

I always thought that I'd be back: riding up front, in charge of the fire appliance as we raced over the Tyne bridge, off to the next battle.

Days came and went and the trial approached. Whilst I had begun to feel fitter, I still looked terrible; gaunt and drawn with patchy skin. I'd put some muscle back on and was back up to twelve stone, twelve pounds, due in no small measure, to my mother's cooking and Paul supplementing me at weekends with a few pints of Guinness.

I felt no sorrow, as my friend Mickey Welford informed me that Tamara was already on another online dating site; '*Wanting to meet someone trustworthy.*' Already onto her next 'mark'.

I kept working on the trial preparation.

We approached Davey Mc. and spoke to him. He told me the same story of the hell she had put him through. Danielle spoke to him too when suddenly, he shat his pants and wouldn't help. I discovered he'd been threatened by Tamara and visited and deterred by DC Darkman. Now everyone has heard of the Mafia threatening prosecution witnesses, but defence witnesses? By the 'victim' and the police?

Suzie also confirmed this: having said she would state that I was not a violent or hateful man, she too was harassed by Tamara and subjected to many phone calls and threats, as well as being pressured by DC Darkman. *See appendix docs

About two weeks before the trial I was out walking Barney when, approaching a T-junction near my dad's, I noticed a car in a layby; the number plate showing 'Benfield Motors', based in the east end of Newcastle. It pulled away towards dad's house, as the old man trudged up and down the grass verge with his decrepit lawnmower. As I approached, the car pulled up and two 'heavies' got out; overweight, big lads who approached my dad with their backs to me. My dad saw me and gave a quick signal with his eye. I hopped over the field gate a bit further down and Barney squeezed through the stile. Zipping around, I ducked through the field and into my dad's; coming up behind his six-foot wooden gate.

'He's not here lads, but you can wait for him if you like, just head through the gates.'

Now, most people generally carry some sort of home protection; in my father's case it was a pick-axe handle, propped just inside the gate. As the gate opened, I swung the shaft low and straight across the first guy's knees. As he buckled underneath himself in agony, my dad dropped the other guy and we dragged him in and locked the gates.

Now, I hadn't heard what was said, but apparently they'd threatened my dad and myself, and I'd been told to plead guilty. That crazy cow had sent some kind of emissaries! As they lay on the floor, probably thirty-five stone of useless blubber, my dad let rip...

'You tell her that if she wants a war, she's got one, and if you ever come back down to Trentside, bring an Army because we'll just keep burying you in the woods. Now fuck off back up north, you pair of fucking idiots.'

Tamara had decided to play dirty, but we were playing

with a straight bat; in both senses of the word, as her hired thugs had found out!

We put our faith into the judicial system; a mistake that I will never make again.

My knowledge of criminal law was, as a layman, as good as it was going to be. I was certain with our defence, we could establish my credibility as a person of good character and the inconsistencies in the statements of the enemy could be exposed. We could even draw them into lying under oath and perjuring themselves; itself a major criminal offence, or felony.

The week came before the trial, Danielle called me; '*The District Judge has fallen down his stairs at home, so the Court wants to proceed with magistrates' overseeing*'.

I was not happy with this at all. Magistrates are 'lay persons', they don't have law degrees but are reliant on advice from a 'Clerk of Justices', which they can take into account or not.

Usually right wing politically, and often wannabe do-gooders, on some kind of mission, they have the power to send people to jail for up to eighteen months.

I was filled with foreboding. Having worked all my life to be a top professional; my future was now in the hands of three amateurs.

'*We still haven't got the interview tapes from your first arrest through, despite us asking for them many times, under the disclosure protocols.*'

Now, in a Crown Court, where 'felonies' or serious offences are heard, a professional judge can dismiss a case immediately on the grounds that police failure to provide crucial evidence can prejudice a trial. What could possibly go wrong?

Chapter 9

Trial - Two Angry Men & a Woman

I was ushered into court and into the dock for the accused by the orderlies at Newcastle Magistrates' Court.

I glanced at the public gallery which was full. This was perhaps the last time I felt real brotherhood within the fire service: my colleagues and friends, both recent and from years before, had all turned up to show solidarity. A few gave me the thumbs up and several others, 'the nod'.

'All rise.'

The three magistrates walked out. The first man was maybe slightly younger than me. The Head magistrate was bearded, small and bespectacled. He was followed by a woman who resembled Theresa May, later to become British Prime Minister.

They looked at me. Bald, drawn, gaunt; drowning in a borrowed suit from one of my good friends the West brothers, Chris and Adam from Whitley Bay.

I felt their prejudice burning into me from their eyes. I imagined them thinking at that moment;

'Looks like a thug... accused of minor violence... this is a done deal.'

The first cross examination began with the CPS lawyer asking me to give accounts for the accusations Tamara had made.

I was desperate to emphasise the points that I knew would be pivotal;

- The nature of the solid door;
- The threats made towards me by Tamara;
- The 'L' shape of the kitchen.
- The amount of money at stake

The lawyer asked me a few ambiguous questions which I asked her to clarify. Unable to do so, she then withdrew them: I was off the stand.

In walked Tamara; expensively dressed, who proceeded to give the most melodramatic performance possibly witnessed in that city (and that includes 'Auf Weidersehen, Pet'). Crying crocodile tears and saying how she had loved me but that I had abused her. She painted me as a big bad wolf; *'He's addicted to steroids and worships Raoul Moat! He hates the police and thinks he can do what he wants because he's a Fireman.'* (There had been a very high-profile case in the area a few years earlier, where an extremely troubled man called Raoul Moat, had killed a number of people, prior to a police chase and suicide. Whilst I don't know the intimate details of that case; as always, there is more to it than was reported in the press.)

The public gallery erupted in laughter at this ridiculous statement and now our barrister started to cross examine; '*You say you were pregnant at the time of the alleged event where he grabbed and threatened you?*'

'*Yes.*'

'*And that was the previous July?*'

'*Yes.*'

'*So, where's the baby?*'

'*I miscarried.*'

'*Well, we have your medical records here and there is no record of any pregnancy, nor any miscarriage. There is also no record of you being admitted to hospital for any treatment.*'

'*Well, I never went.*'

'*So, you are telling me that you miscarried, which can kill women from blood loss but you sought no medical attention? I find that very difficult to believe.*'

Jackpot... Now she was caught in a lie: the bit was between the teeth. The whole court waited for the barrister to go for the kill: to keep going; to force the admission... but she didn't. She just gave a knowing look to the bench instead.

Now, I have no doubt that a District Judge would have fully understood and acknowledged this look and its subtle implication, and probably thrown the case out at that stage: but it was apparently too subtle for these magistrates.

This pattern repeated itself: the initial arresting officer was challenged on her ability to see through solid wooden doors but again, this was not hammered home. Once a layout of the house was produced, Davis Peters was shown to have been unable to see around corners, as he'd claimed he had done. Tamara's mother gave a completely different version of events to her daughter.

Each time the barrister gave the bench a knowing look and rolled her eyes... surely this was enough?

During all this time Tamara, unlike most 'victims', chose to sit in the public gallery and continued her dramatic performance; wiping the crocodile tears, shaking her head and interrupting... The usual behavior from someone who has allegedly been so intimidated that they could hardly go out!

Butler stepped up to give evidence, stating that he had witnessed Tamara assaulting and verbally abusing me. Suzie went on record saying that in all the years we had been together, at no time did I ever use any violence or threatening behavior towards her.

Kevin Totton, likewise, stated that he had witnessed Tamara verbally berating and hitting me.

As we waited in the Bacchus pub, a stone's throw from the court, I shook everyone's hand and thanked them for the support. This was a done deal: the prosecution witnesses all been shown to be liars, the police embarrassed and incompetent.

'See you back at work next week then?'

An hour passed; then two; then three; then four; then five... What the fuck was going on?

Danielle called and said; '*Right, they're going to be ready with a verdict. It's in the bag...*'

We walked back over but as we arrived, Danielle said; '*Something odd has just happened: they asked to see DC Darkman on his own; that's highly irregular.*'

We walked back into court, I stood in the dock and the magistrates entered.

'We have discussed this at length and although we don't believe all that the prosecution have alleged: we don't believe

all the defence has said either... Given that - we find the accused guilty. He should return for sentencing in twenty-eight days.'

I felt as though I'd been punched in the guts. Total disbelief and disgust. The law states that if there is any way a crime is not proved beyond reasonable doubt, then the accused should be afforded the benefit of that doubt. The magistrates had acknowledged that the burden of proof had not been reached but they found against me anyway!

The public gallery was filled with boos and hisses, while Tamara threw her arms in the air in victory. The Clerk of Justices looked at Danielle with her palms upturned and shrugged her shoulders, shaking her head.

Davis Peters, looked over and winked, before making the 'Wanker' gesture at me.

DC Darkman laughed at me and said; '*You lot are all the same. Nothing but a thick fireman!*'

Things would never be the same again. I was taken through to sign some documents and bail forms to return for sentencing. As I prepared to leave for the long drive back to Trentside, I was approached by two police officers and asked to leave via the police station.

Apparently, Tamara and her supporters were standing outside the court, goading and gloating; verbally abusing the fire service staff attending and wanting an altercation.

Scum. Sub-human scum.

As dad and I drove down the A1 past Leeming Bar, I turned to him and said; '*We've had worse days!*'

He laughed, knowing that although I'd been beaten, I wasn't broken.

After the initial shock, I had to get down to business: I knew that being found guilty of a criminal act would give more than sufficient grounds for a gross misconduct dismissal from the fire service. Although so many were present and they all knew this was a huge miscarriage of justice, like a soccer result; the score stands for perpetuity rather than the quality of the performance.

Despite the fact that; **I had been convicted of a crime for which there was no record provided that I had even been interviewed about!**

The recordings of the interview of the 6th October, where Steve Davis articulated the lies of the arresting officer and her allegedly X-Ray vision, had mysteriously not been provided; despite many requests by Danielle Jackson (see appendix)

Now, the police are in a difficult situation with regard to this case.

Should there be sufficient public interest to look into these proceedings again, it can be seen in two ways: if the recordings of that interview now 'appear', it would certainly look like the police deliberately concealed them from the trial in order to influence the result to that which they wanted.

On the other hand: should the status quo be upheld and the recordings remain lost, then I have been convicted, without any record of me being interviewed in regard to the alleged events; so that any testimony related to that by said police officers, should be inadmissible in court!

I'm not saying that they're completely corrupt but at the very least, the situation described makes them look grossly unprofessional and incompetent!

Danielle wrote a letter (see appendix) where she advised us of our options. She had spoken with the chief fire officer, explaining the circumstances of the trial in detail and he had given his word that I would not be dismissed.

To appeal the case would cost around £25,000; money that I simply did not have. Danielle considered that, having fired all of our ammunition, at any appeal hearing; the opposition would know our approach and tighten up their testimonies to seem more convincing and it would be unlikely that we would alter the outcome. Seeing as the sentence was community banded, her opinion was to put this behind us; do some litter picking and move forward. Get divorced and resume my career. That sounded reasonable.

As I approached the court for the sentencing hearing, I saw Tamara on the far side of the road talking to another woman who promptly walked towards me and stuck a camera in my face. She had only invited the local press!

Sentenced to 100 hours community service, I walked out of the court and got down to brass tacks: I needed to go to Headquarters.

Sitting outside the chief's office, I had already typed my resignation letter. Although Danielle had been given an assurance that I would not be dismissed, I could have no complaints if I was asked to resign. Wrongly or not, I had been convicted of a crime and that was grounds for dismissal.

I walked into his office, came to attention and saluted; '*Sit down.*' I did so; a million thoughts running through my head: was this the end of my career?

'You look like shit. I've also heard that you've given half your wages whilst suspended to charity, since we wouldn't take them back?'

'I don't think it's right to take money I haven't worked for Sir.'

'Well, I think you've been through enough shite, so get out of here for a month and then come back to work. You'll be

off the tools for a bit and you'll not be promoted again for a few years but that will pass: today's news is tomorrow's fish and chip paper.'

As I walked through the open plan office at Headquarters, I could feel the eyes burning in my back. I still had my job and perhaps I could recover from this.

Chapter 10

Picking up the Pieces (of poo)

I attended my first day of community service in Wallsend, North Tyneside. Registration prior to litter-picking in the municipal park: no problem. As I left the Office and turned into Station Road.

'Get on with your punishment you cunt!'

I looked up. Tamara and her mother, laughing and sneering: not only had she stitched me up, now they'd come to revel in it: for entertainment.

'I've ruined your life and now I'm going to take your money!'

'Why don't you just fuck off? My only regret now is that I didn't touch you. At least if I had I'd have had some satisfaction!' I responded, goaded into stupidity.

The Supervisor noted this and came over. Words were spoken and then I was walked back to the Probation office next to Wallsend Metro station and given a phone; Danielle on the other end.

'You're being transferred to the Staffordshire and West Midlands Probation service and doing your community service down there.

There's a special riding school in a small place called Scropton, in east Staffordshire. They provide riding lessons for disabled kids and adults, with stables of around twenty-five horses. There are a number of Category D, open prisons nearby, where prisoners nearing the end their sentence, can transition back into civilian life by attending for work albeit unpaid, each day.

We were now into the late spring and the first rays of summer shone through the blue sky and ice cream clouds. The second order of the day after clearing the stables, was to barrow the horse manure up to the fields and dump it into two large trailers which then went to a nearby farmer for fertiliser. A mind-numbingly boring operation; the horses seemed to shit as quick as we could fill the trailers.

After a couple of days of this, I sat in the canteen with the rest of the workers, a mixture of long-term lifers, those ready for release and community service statistics like myself.

'It's a nice day, wouldn't you rather be sitting down waiting for the trailers to get back, doing some bronzing?'

'Only one trailer goes out at a time you clown., one of the lifers on day release replied; *'Not if we fill both of them at the same time...' 'How do you mean?' 'Well if we work our bollocks off for an hour or so first thing and fill them both, they'll have to fuck off together and we'll have no more work to do... you see?' 'Ok' 'So are you up for it then?' 'Why not? I wasn't off to see my Accountant'*

Pairing up and rotating quickly, we began the next day at a good pace; running back and forth under the morning sun as the trailers began to fill up with horse-shit. After about two hours, both trailers were full and we all sat down, backed up against a three-bar fence; some with shirts off as the sun reached its highest point.

'Why are you lot sitting down?' Stuart, the facility manager and ex-Guards officer came over and asked.

'Both trailers are full Stuart.' 'How can that be? it's normally one in the morning and one in the afternoon.' 'Well, they're both full of crap. Much like my ex-wife.' cue a few sniggers;

'Oh, very well.'

The trailer took about an hour-and-a-half to get back and as the stables were cleaned and the poo picked, there wasn't an awful lot to do. I sat and watched some of these men: guys who'd had their liberty taken from them, and thought to myself - what if some of these guys were innocent too? What if they'd gotten a similarly shit decision in court? They walked round, tops off, breathing in the late spring air, some stroking the horses; feeling like free men. Men with a choice: if only for a few brief hours.

The phone disturbed my moment. Keith Ladler, a firefighter who I'd had relatively little to do with was on the end of the line: he'd never rung me before, so this was strange.

'You're on the cover of the Chronicle.'

Tamara had spoken to the regional rag, the Newcastle Evening Chronicle, who hadn't even attended the court, only the sentencing. She detailed how I had allegedly ruined her life, providing a photo from my own collection, taken when we'd rescued a boxer dog, from the picket lines in the 2002 strikes.

The headline in the print edition read; **Hero Fireman is vile Wife-Beating Thug.**

Not just in the rag: the Chronicle had recently gone online as well, so this gutter journalism would be available on the internet forever. The realisation didn't really kick right then but this hate-filled diatribe, would impact the rest of my life.

'Keith, I've been picking up shit for the last few days. But you've paid 50pence to do that with that rag. Thanks for the call.' I hung up.

I never stayed in touch with any of the lads I did community service with, or from the prison. I felt it was a moment in time which passed and while I still feel that there are many victims of the judicial system, I had to begin to be more generous and selfless in my own outlook - to improve.

Chapter 11

D.I.V.O.R.C.E.

As you can imagine dear hearts, my faith in the UK judicial process was diminishing as rapidly as my faith in humanity. To top this off; I was now going through the divorce process.

Put simply, there are three levels: an agreement is reached by a couple and then the court formalizes it. If that doesn't happen, cases are stated in front of a judge who then gives a verdict on how they believe an agreement should be made. If this is not agreed with, then a formal hearing commences, with horse-trading under a judge's advice until a decision can be imposed.

Tamara, of course, had stated that there would be no agreement and that she was entitled to 100%, as I was apparently a; '*Wife Beating Thug who has ruined my life.*' She also refused to appear in any mediation hearing, so it was at the court stage where our paths crossed for the final time.

The protagonists were Tamara and her lawyer, an outwardly disheveled looking, but very sharp guy called Liam Ford, who was held in high regard on Tyneside, versus myself and the dapper Robert Coles, a Leeds-based divorce barrister, who had retired from criminal defence law having never lost a case, and moved into the lucrative world of family law. The two sides were diametrically opposed: this was Tyneside versus Trentside and a lot of money was at stake.

Unusually they were already sat in the room when we arrived; as the judge entered from chambers and we all stood.

Ford said; '*Apologies your honour but my client is unable to stand due to a medical condition.*'

'*Very well.*' the lady judge replied.

The opening exchanges were to be as expected: production of the gutter press article and a detailed explanation of the way Tamara had allegedly been 'left in fear' and permanently damaged by her seven-week marriage to me. Then the 'coup-de-gras'.

'*She has been so damaged by this man, that she is unable to have relationships with other men and it is unlikely that she ever will. She should be compensated for that and awarded 100%.*'

I snorted in derision, I have to admit. Having looked at her social media and reports in from my colleagues like Mickey who had seen her on the dating website, I knew for a fact that she'd been out revelling most weekends and had been actively online dating whilst I was on bail, awaiting trial. As she'd become a known, notorious figure due to the amount of malicious complaints, there had been many sightings from my former colleagues.

Mr Coles took a far more methodical approach and examined the cold facts. He detailed the percentage of money bought by both parties into assets, the short length of marriage, the fact that her allegations were still denied and plenty of them had been proved untrue. However, this did not seem to be resonating with the lady judge. I felt the glare of prejudice burning into me once again, my bald, de-pigmented scalp and poorly fitting clothes being viewed as the uniform of the thug Fireman.

Ford opened the trading; 90%, 10%: Coles responded in kind. As this went on and on, both sides refused to budge from a 75%/25% judgment in their favour. This was coming down to the judge.

Outside the room Mr Ford, alone, looked at myself and Coles and spoke; '*This is fucking outrageous and I'm professionally embarrassed to do this, but I've got to follow my client's orders and she wants to take this down to the last £20. Do yourself a favour and choose a better one for your next ex-wife son!*'

'*We'd better go to the judge then.*' replied Mr Coles.

'*Given that Mr Walker has very good job security and will probably end his career as a senior fire officer on an excellent pension, it is considered that Tamara Walker will receive 75% of the joint assets: not including the disputed £40k, which she is entitled to keep.*'

Mr Coles looked in disbelief, Mr Ford likewise. Tamara smirked and the judge ordered this to be written up and agreed.

As Tamara stood up, the large camel-hair coat she'd kept on during the whole day fell open, revealing a visible baby bump.

'*So afraid of other men, she's up the stick by one your honour. Where's your justice now? You're as wrong as those magistrates: a bunch of fucking amateurs.*'

The judge turned away and marched out. Under normal circumstances, I would have been considered in contempt of court and locked up. But she knew I was right.

Outside, Mr Coles came over to me. Opening his wallet, he reached a wad of notes out; £250.

'*You've been royally shafted by that woman, so at the very least take your mates out for a curry or something. I saw you play rugby once at Huddersfield years ago. Should have played for England.'*

'I'd rather have your fountain pen.'

He reached into his tailored three-piece pinstripe suit and pulling out a silver fountain pen, he placed it in my pocket. My legal fees were astronomical. After I had paid these, less the amount granted by divorce I had seven grand to start a new life. At least I had my job. That was something.

Chapter 12

Back to Work, then Gone

No sooner had I got back to Tyneside than I was in the back of a police car. Arrested and accused of apparently threatening to kill Tamara and her new partner (who had allegedly corroborated this). My being 200 miles away at the time of the alleged event was no impediment for her and whilst a more senior police officer commented that, unless I had a helicopter, the time frames didn't add up, I was straight back into the twenty-three hours detention.

This continued and continued, until a line was drawn: I was invited up to the principal officer's suite and sat down; *'We're advising you to transfer out son. We're sorry but we're losing too much time every occasion she clicks her fingers and has you nicked.'*

I found out later that allegedly a petition had been circulated, signed by a number of female staff in the brigade, saying that they felt uncomfortable that someone convicted of domestic violence offences was in the same workplace. Gossiping, ignorant harridans: an early indication of the prejudice that I would now face daily.

To their utmost credit, I was told that not one female firefighter or member of Control Staff in the brigade signed that document (to my knowledge) and the senior officers nipped it in the bud, making it very clear that this was discrimination and would be treated as harassment. A statement in every way.

Nobody was looking for transfers in. Potential exchanges were mooted then fell through to Derbyshire, Staffordshire, West Midlands.

Eventually a county fire brigade (name changed) came up; 'Watch and Crew' managers wanted. About forty miles from my parents and the location seemed acceptable. Phone calls were made by the chief and the paperwork was done: the worst mistake of my professional career.

I cleared my locker out into a large box, looked at my gear and thought, One box for a lifetime.

I slung a copy of FIRE magazine on the top of it and a leaflet fell out; 'We need your help. The International Fire Rescue Association (IFRA) supplies equipment and training to firefighters in third world countries where crews are wearing denim coats and gardening gloves whilst trying to protect their communities.'

Interested, I read on; the organization based in Scotland, was completely self-funding and had at that time, given help in seven or eight countries. There was a telephone number at the bottom of the leaflet: I called it and introduced myself, explaining that I was in a state of transition but wished to help; *'I'll get you on the email list and just do what you can, when you can son'.* A friendly Scottish brogue on the end of the phone: a voice I would come to know well.

I reported to where I had been told to on the joining instructions. I walked into the station manager's office, knocked on the door and entered; *'I'm Ben Walker, transferred from Tyne & Wear Metropolitan. Nice to meet you'.*

I put my hand out.

As the kids say these days, I was 'left hanging' with the refusal to shake my outstretched hand.

Tom Christmas sat behind his desk shuffling some papers, including a print-out of the hatchet job the Newcastle Chronicle had done on me, portraying me as some kind of maniac and opened his mouth. The smell of cigarettes and halitosis was pungent as he tried to fix me with a stare and said;

'I never interviewed you, I don't want people like you in my district and as far as I'm concerned you are here because of politics between chief officers returning favours.'

'Well, I'm here anyway. I always give 100% and if you don't like that, I'm not going to lose any sleep about it.' I'd moved from the north east to get away from this hostility, yet my first encounter was full of confrontation. I knew this was going to be a bad move.

I got posted to a small town, let's call it Stoneacre, which had been a village fire station that had grown slightly in size but still remained community-based. I arrived with another transferee called Karl, who'd returned from a career break in the west Midlands and had also been a metropolitan firefighter.

I can only say that it was like stepping back in time twenty years: with the exception of an old sweat called Robin Red Breast, the interaction and banter was out of touch to say the least. Stuff that was totally unacceptable in the metropolitan brigades flew freely here; racist terms, Paki jokes, gay people referred to as fudge-packers; all in daily use. Disgusting and unacceptable. Always was, always will be.

Kenny Davidson, my old divisional officer in the north, told me several years before, when I got my first promotion; *'What you permit, you promote...'* '

And I certainly didn't promote this type of attitude. I challenged the homophobic remarks made on the station one day; '*You cannot say this stuff. It's fucking offensive.*' '*Why, are you a puff or something?*'

This is what I was dealing with. Already viewed with suspicion, arising from my large operational experience gained on the mean streets of the north east, this put my head firmly above the parapet.

There were a few younger guys, not beyond redemption, but easily led by the shit outlook and ethics of those ensconced: one such example was the smoking crew.

I have never smoked but I understand that people do; it's personal choice and a freedom. However, this station took things to extremes. It takes what, seven or eight minutes to smoke a cigarette? With a leisurely walk to and from the smoking area, often with a coffee as well, each cigarette was costing fifteen minutes a time.

Time, in which the younger, more easily dominated guys were continuing to work, cleaning and testing equipment. Some easy mental mathematics at ten cigarettes a day, meant the smokers were taking two and a half hours on the company; ten hours a week: a whole working week in each four. Accounting for leave, these guys were spending ten or so weeks a year smoking rather than working.

I made it clear that I thought this was unfair on the other firefighters and that smoking should only take place within the standard breaks. A backlash came from Tom Christmas, a heavy smoker himself, who overruled me and accused me of causing trouble.

As the weather deteriorated, I could see that not only did this continue unabated but the piss was being well and truly taken. I spotted a smoke-detector cover had appeared in the men's toilets and a few dog-ends were beginning to turn up in the toilet bowls. Christmas certainly promoted this, despite it being illegal since 2006 to smoke in a workplace (Health Act 2006). Over the next few days I noticed the little tobacco club, including Christmas himself sneaking off down to the lavs (heads in the US) to indulge.

It would be irresponsible for me to tell you which, but if two popular and widely available domestic cleaning products are mixed and diluted with water, they will give off a flammable gas. Usually this mixes with air pretty quickly and disperses but in the right concentrations and within the right ratio of air, it will ignite explosively.

Bringing in the cleaning products, I waited for days until a wet morning: looking outside, I could see the smoking shelter in a deluge. Slipping off to the lavs, I mixed the cleaning products and poured them into the bowl, giving the water a quick stir. I pulled some kitchen wrap tight over the bowl and dropped the seat; I didn't want the now potent mix dispersing.

Slipping round into the next stall, I locked the door and climbed over the top, leaving the one cubicle only: as I walked out of the corridor, I saw the smoking gang led by Christmas, coming towards me. Even having the audacity to reach for their fag packets as they passed me in the narrow passage.

What happened next, I can only guess at, but given the running exodus and smell of burning around ten minutes later I can fill in the gaps... Lighting up, they'd gathered in their little coven, smoking away and talking shit, probably slagging me off: then they'd gone to dispose the dog-ends into a toilet bowl. With only one cubicle in action they'd have lifted the lid and found the cling-film, either removing it or burning through it; the lit butt ends providing the ignition source the flammable mixture was waiting for;.... Whoosh!

As they ran out, embarrassed, shocked and sheepish, Christmas glared at me and said;

'Did you have anything to do with this?' 'Well, they do say smoking is bad for your health.'

'I'm going to get you Walker.' 'I Don't want to disappoint you, but I've heard that before.'

Operationally, the county crews I personally encountered (which by no means was all of those serving in that brigade) were poor by comparison to the crews I'd previously worked with back up in the north east. This isn't sour grapes or bitterness but they seemed so inexperienced and lacking in drive or motivation by comparison with my former colleagues. While a lot of the blame for this can be laid at the door of questionable, outdated procedures and lackluster training, it was also due to the fear environment they worked in, with some noted bullies in their chain of command. Christmas, Gabble, Baleman; men who would never have made those positions in large city brigades.

I attended a BA 'refresher' course, and one simulation was to rescue a 'Firefighter down', from a basement situation: paired up with a less physically adept crew member, I bore the brunt of the weight and dragged the simulated casualty out... To my surprise, some days later, I was accused of 'Injuring an instructor's back' during an exercise. Ironically, I myself was suffering a recurrent back pain and asked a visiting brigade nurse for a quick opinion on my sacroiliac injury. This was 'spun' by Christmas into to some kind of 'exposing oneself' or 'mooning' at the brigade nurse! I felt like I was playing against a rigged deck every day, in every way.

However, finding solutions is my game, not listing my problems. I began to work on ways to improve things. I compiled a large list to start chipping away at, starting with Fire Science. I dug out some old training notes we'd used at Gateshead and put them out for reference, proposing a quiz in a couple of weeks with a prize... Within hours, this had been returned with;

Not the official view of County FRS. Do not Read!
in thick black marker pen.

How the laws of physics and chemistry were not the official fire service view, still astounds me to this day. In a sharp twist of irony, this document eventually evolved into my first book 'Fire Dynamics for firefighters', which the Institute of Fire Engineers endorses and every UK fire service now has to use for training purposes.

Almost overnight, the floodgates opened. I had proactively challenged bad attitudes, bad behavior, poor training and operations: not in order to make anyone look bad but to make things better; for the firefighters and for the communities they represented.

Mail began to arrive at the station for me through the internal post. A succession of anti-domestic violence posters with '***Fuck off back North and beat your wife***' written on them in marker pen arrived.

The online version of the Evening Chronicle's article about me, '***Hero Fireman is Vile Thug!***' was also distributed and pinned up on station noticeboards, and often left for weeks on display. What you permit, you promote: so apparently this behaviour was not only tolerated but promoted!

On the rare occasions we did attend incidents or other fire stations, verbal abuse from other (male) firefighters, including one officer who now holds a very high rank in the fire department;

'*Are you the Geordie wifebeater*?' Replying with a succinct; '*Marry me and find out, you cunt!*' was responded to with a formal complaint about me being abusive to them!

Around this time, I also got a call from an old buddy; Percy Johnson, in Tyne & Wear, who the County Fire Service were using as a training provider, to send staff to qualify as instructors;

'Are you ok mate?'

'Usual shit, different day: why do you ask?'

'Got some clown from your new service up here on a course I'm on. He's slagging you off unmercifully and saying you'd been suspended from work for touching kids on a school visit!'

'What the fuck? That's absolute bollocks'

'Well, we all thought that. I'll put the prick straight in the morning.'

Not only were these arseholes trying to destroy my career, they were going up North and trying to ruin what personal standing I had left. What a pack of bastards!

I was renting a room from a guy called Sean, who was a retained firefighter in the County Fire Service. I found out later through a phone call and then a Whatsapp message (appendix), that he was being leaned on to report back anything that I.said or did whilst off-duty. With the carrot of a full-time job being dangled in front of him, he was supposed to report back to Christmas and the others at the fire station. Unfortunately for them, I'm a man of integrity and he had nothing to report.

However, the County Fire Service was breaching my Human Rights: illegal surveillance, bullying and harassing. Was this a fire department or some kind of Stasi/Gestapo outfit? It was getting ridiculous: I began to reach out to the union, or trying to. I sent emails, text messages and left voicemails - over forty - with no response. The Fire Brigade's Union were selling me down the river! Where was the help I was entitled to as a paying member? I had to draw the line and accept that things were never going to work out here.

I rang up Shane McQueen; '*You can take a horse to water but can't make it drink! The yokels probably aren't ready for a force of nature like you. They're pissed off because you've got more experience, you're better trained, you know more, you're better looking, you're sexier and you've had hundreds more lasses than them!*'

He was being flippant but the underlying message was right: I had to transfer out.

I went to see Christmas, who promptly denied my request, stating that I was his, to do with what he liked: what a complete prick!

Getting no response from the union, I spoke to my cousin Martin, a watch manager in Leicestershire. He spoke to his union rep Art Tenant, who called me and asked what was going on: he told me I needed to get out of there.

A week before the Christmas holiday, I was called into a meeting with Christmas and a small, nervous looking girl; '*It's been decided that County are terminating your contract. As you've been here less than twelve months, changing employer to our County Council from Tyne & Wear Fire & Civil Defence Authority, you technically have no employment protection; continuity of service being only for pay and pension purposes. So unpack your locker and get out.'*

Christmas smirked; he couoldn't challenge me on any performance issues so, covering his own flaws, he had managed to bullet me on a technicality! Surely the Union wouldn't allow this?

***In his personal defence, Brad Moore of the Fire Brigades' Union did take up some dialogue with the County Fire Service's HR department but hit brick walls everywhere. Following this, I wrote on several occasions to the national executive council and General Secretary of The Fire Brigades' Union to find out why, when I had reached out to union officials within the County (Brad Moore was a regional official presiding above them) over 40 times, I had had no response. To date this issue remains unresolved and no explanation has yet been provided by the Fire Brigades' Union.**

Chapter 13

Daniel Blake and I

Walking Barney around Jackson's Bank that afternoon, I was relieved that I was no longer forced to work in that toxic atmosphere with amateurs, bunglers and idlers. I also felt confident that the Union would be outraged and create hell and that I'd be rapidly transferred over to a Metropolitan Brigade, like the renowned West Midland Fire Service and the hotspots of Birmingham and the Black Country.

It did worry me that I'd had no replies from any the union officials in the County, but Art Tennant had contacted the West Midlands region through the East Midlands office of the union and a chap called Brad Moore came to see me, meeting at a solicitor's office in Birmingham;

'This stinks to high heaven and is clearly an unfair dismissal.' said the lawyer *'However, your change of employer and the less than twelve months service there, means we can't take it to tribunal. I'm sorry.'*

So, there was nothing I could do. I sat with Brad and wrote an official compliant, asking for reasons why the County union officials had not responded to any of my requests for help. To date, in 2018, I still haven't received a reply, despite the upper echelons of the Union's Head Office being asked for it.

Not happy with just seeing me lose my livelihood, the kind souls at County got their friend and colleague from Hampton Fire Service, to call every HR dept in every local brigade, to state that I was an unsavoury person, a wife-beating bastard and should not be engaged with.

Mud Sticks; as I found out.

I must have telephoned, emailed and written to every fire service in the UK. Always the same response;

'As you are no longer in continuous service, we are unable to accept your transfer request'

Usually signed by some HR assistant with limited understanding of the real qualities of a firefighter rather than those on a checklist.

I decided I needed to speak to the 'organ grinders' and began to ring a few of the chiefs directly, trying to explain the circumstances. Most were so politically savvy, they referred me back straight to HR. One or two though, were still in touch with the shop floor and one Metropolitan Department chief did have the decency to speak to me;

*'I know all about you son- it's been discussed at CFOA (*Chiefs' Association*), and personally I think what you've been through is shit. I have no doubt that I could put you in charge of my busiest station and that you'd do a brilliant job. However... As soon as you piss someone off, what d'you think will happen? I'll have the City Mail and the Express & Star headlining that a convicted bastard is running one of our top stations. That's something that we cannot get over these days. I'm very sorry.'*

It hit me like a ton of bricks, although I appreciated the honesty, however brutal. Mulling this over I walked to the shop to get some milk for the great British tradition of a cup of tea;

'Sorry Sir, your card's been declined.

Embarrassed, I apologized and walked away. I knew that funds were running low: ever since that divorce fiasco, I'd been living week to week on my salary, whilst paying off debts and I'd finally hit zero; without a pot to piss in.

I went through the process and arranged an appointment to sign on the dole for a Jobseeker's allowance (known as Welfare in the US).

The Unemployment Benefits Office in Burton is sited in the most visible position possible. Right outside the entrance to the Coopers Square Shopping Centre. As I stood in the queue outside, I battled with my ego. Like the Angel and Devil in the cartoons, half of me hoped nobody would see me, I was embarrassed and somewhat ashamed; whilst my other half me was telling me, I'd nothing to be ashamed about: I was here through no real fault of my own, just the confluence of a number of bad circumstances.

To my shame in previous years, I'd always regarded unemployment as the choice of the lazy and work-shy. The childhood image of all those dads watching the school football match with no jobs to go to, flitted through my mind. But now I was in their shoes.

A kindly chap called Glynn was the Job Seeker's coach: I'd been asked to take a CV and reading through it, he looked me in the eye and asked;

'How did you end up here?'

'Bad luck, crap circumstance and the wrong woman'

'Many are victims of the latter of those three.'

Glynn explained the protocols: apply for twenty jobs a week, document the evidence and report o sign on each fortnight. Simple enough I thought: I wasn't intending on being here longer than necessary.

As I picked up the paperwork to leave, a young man, maybe twenty-six or seven got up from an adjacent desk. As we got to the door together, he turned to me and asked;

'Can you do me a favour mate, please?'

'Yeah, no problem.'

'Can you explain this to me?' handing me the same piece of paper; *'I don't read too well'*

'OK mate'

Ricky had been a bit of a rogue all his life: from a vicious and abusive background, he'd drifted into a cycle of truancy from school into petty crime, substance abuse and repeated jail time. But he'd asked me politely. I bought us a cup of coffee and sat down with him to explain the details: he expressed his fear of being 'sanctioned' for not being able to complete the job applications because of his literacy issues.

'I want to stay off the gear and keep clean but if I get my dole stopped, then I've no option but to start dealing again or starve.'

And I thought that I didn't have many choices.

Over the following few weeks, I met Ricky twice a week at the library and helped him with job applications and reading. We'd sit in a quiet area and pick up a book; nothing too patronizing but something simple to read. We worked on sentence structure and practiced some basic interview techniques: situation - action - task- result-type answers: I watched his confidence grow.

'I've got an interview tomorrow at Clipper (Warehouse).'

'Brilliant mate'

'Thanks for your help mate, I'll let you know how it goes..'

'GOT JOB!! SEE YOU SOON', came the text message.

I never saw Ricky again but I hope he got himself sorted. It gave me the hope though, that it wasn't too late to save myself, I just had to stop saving others, but the firefighter creed ran deep through my blood.

My days now consisted of long walks, job applications and reading. I'd started really dissecting all firefighting training material during my period on bail and now with time on my hands, I kicked into overdrive; Braidwood, Tozer, Grimwood. I pored over all the manuals and made meticulous notes: If I couldn't actually be in the job, I was surely going to know more about than anyone else!

If you can't join them, beat them: after a few hours reading, I would compose emails to various manufacturers, suppliers and fire services, requesting donations on behalf of the International Fire Rescue Charity. I couldn't do much myself but I could spend an hour a day trying to get stuff from those that could.

Most job applications didn't even get responded to. Weeks passed and yet more applications were sent, until I finally got a call back from a warehouse.

'We'd like to thank you for your application, but we Googled you and don't think you're suitable as a lot of women work here'.

I don't know if it's standard nowadays to do a background check but I knew that anyone looking at me online would find that newspaper article, portraying me as a power-drill-wielding madman who apparently threatens pregnant women. And nobody would even bother to ask my side of the story, let alone listen. That article returns again and again to haunt me, all based on lies: the reporter didn't even go to the trial.

The job applications passed 300, then 400, then 500, and kept going up to 800: unwanted.

Was this my destiny? To be a loser in life?

At this point, I'd been evicted from my digs as I couldn't afford to pay the rent. I'd foreseen it happening and had the decency to tell the landlord.

With nowhere to turn and after a spell sleeping rough, I was camping in my dad's garage, there being very few rooms in his little place. I began to feel worse and worse; phone cut off, no money to see any friends, all my old work pals 200 miles away.

'Would anyone miss me if I wasn't here? Would anyone care?'

I began to work out the best ways of killing myself. Unable to master the noose knot, I worked out that a rolling hitch would be easy to tie and non-slip: it would do the job.

I resolved that this was the way to go: full of bitterness, regret and angst, I decided that tonight was the night.

A suicide note would be wasted; I had nothing to say. With tears streaming down my face I picked up the rope.

Barney must have thought that this was his cue for a walk, and my hangman's rope just another dog lead. Jumping up at me he looked me in the eyes and seemed to know: I stared lost into his big brown eyes and it was as if he was communicating telepathically with me.

'Daddy, don't leave me. Daddy don't do this.'

I broke down in tears on the floor, sobbing uncontrollably. Barney, who the evil Tamara had threatened to kill, had just saved my life. I made a solemn promise, that as long as I had Barney to care for, I would never hurt myself or leave him.

As I looked up, I saw my sole poster on the wall, Stallone's opus Rocky Balboa, looking out from the top of the steps of the Philadepphia Art Museum in silhouette: the caption reads;

'It ain't over 'til it's over'

At that moment that in Rocky's own words I knew that;

'It's not about how hard you can hit, but how hard you can get hit, and keep moving forward, how much you can take and keep moving forward.'

Well I'd taken some shit, but I had to keep moving forward. Rather than St Florian, Rocky Balboa would be the unlikely patron saint of this firefighter.

Chapter 14

The Black Labour Market

Being poor in Britain is tough: really tough. The right-wing press and sections of society like to demonise the poor as some form of underclass and the big corporations profit from this. I was about to find out how.

If you wait at 5am by a certain budget supermarket in Burton Upon Trent, the minibuses arrive and out step two or three men: others there stand in a line as these men choose who they want for a day's work. The minibuses take those selected to various construction sites, usually in or around Birmingham: on arrival, you're dished out a hardhat and a high-viz bib. No checks of CSCS cards, no union, no health & safety induction; nothing.

I was so desperate at times that I too, would be waiting in that queue and being a strong, well-muscled lad, I'd invariably get picked. So off I'd go: mixing cement, carrying blocks, bricks and planks each day. I visualized the hard work I was doing paying off as extra training, for the day I would be back saving lives. Deluded maybe but it got me through it: arriving back at around 7pm, each of the workers would be handed a £20 note.

If you read certain newspapers in the UK they will have you believe that immigrants to this country are handed a life of riley on a silver platter. Well that's one of the biggest myths going. It's tough for them: often in condemned or substandard accommodation, often with traumatised children. Escaping from war-torn countries, speaking virtually no English; survival is their only objective.

Whilst waiting in the line, I noted a youngish guy, about 5'6', scrawny and obviously foreign. Some days he'd wait with his wife, who wore a headscarf and held a baby in a papoose around her chest. He wasn't often picked: I mean, looking at him, you'd think a stiff breeze would blow him over. Every day, he seemed to get thinner and thinner, until one day he was picked. Sitting next to him in the mini-bus I asked him his name;

'Achmed'

'Where are you from?'

'Seeria.' (Syria)

From a few moments talking to him it was obvious that this guy and his family were lost in the bureaucracy of the system, living in a building in an area we knew as The Pits, from back when we were kids: it had been due to be condemned before being used to house these poor asylum seekers.

It's an old cliché but the saying; 'There's always somebody worse off than you' never rang as true as it did right then. Nobody was giving this guy any help: I too, had nothing to give but despite this, I had to try.

'*You, you, you and you..* The minibus driver pointed at three guys and me, leaving only Achmed waiting; '*You take him too.'* I gestured towards Achmed; *'No.' 'Well it's both of us, or I don't go.'* Reluctantly the driver agreed and off we went to work.

I kept this up every time I went down there for work: I knew that the men running these crews were coining in serious money and £20 wasn't going to dent their pocket but it meant a lot to this man, so he could care for his family.

Now maybe you'll read this and think all of that's illegal; he's just helped large companies take advantage of the poor: he's helped a guy avoid paying tax through illegal, cash earnings. I make no apology for it though: when you've got absolutely nothing, life becomes about day to day survival. Having just enough to feed your kids; to keep the heating on. If a law has to be broken to ensure that, then so be it. I may have lost everything else, but I hadn't lost my humanity.

It was around this time that I had an email from a fire service in the north of England asking me whether I would be prepared to work in a 'contingency' role as a 'district officer' for times of industrial action. It was heavily implied that this could be a potential route back into the job.

I won't deny that the temptation was strong. It would have been very easy to take the several hundred pounds per shift that was offered, and the Fire Brigades' Union had let me down badly: I owed them nothing. But how could I do it, whilst the people I'd worked with, lived with; were striking for pensions and better conditions?

I wanted to be back but not like that: If I was ever to go back, it would be with my head high, not skulking in by the back door. I chose the poverty I was in. However, I did write the chief fire officer in question a polite letter declining his offer: I knew that was the right thing to do.

Simultaneously, back in Tyne & Wear, a number of officers left the union and worked through the industrial action. By now, Churchers had retired, and the new chief, was dangling promotion carrots to those who wanted to take the bait.

The first name on that list was Walton, the guy who'd shafted me. In disgust at the whole situation, Kenny

Davidson announced his impending retirement: speaking on the phone he said to me;

'The whole regime has no credibility. Promoting only the ones who leave the union. It stinks.

Walton is showing his true colours.'

'You're right. Now I know times are tough for you kid: I know it's harder than anything you've ever been through. But you'll make it. You're made of iron. You're ten times the man that those clowns are.'

Now I don't do anything for plaudits but the decisions we make in life can echo through eternity. I'd never betrayed anyone: my loyalty to the firefighter's code was tested but intact.

Chapter 15

An Examination of Oneself

Sitting at the computer in the library yet again; the perfunctory applications and rejections to be filled in and logged to maintain my dole. I checked my email; 'IFE exams - register now': I looked at the cost - £90. I'd taken the old Fire Service Exam Board statutories when I was younger but I hadn't been tested since. Would I still cut the mustard?

I had a difficult choice to make, Jobseekers Allowance was £71.40 per week: if I took these exams I'd be hungry for a week and have £50 to see me through a fortnight. Any sensible person would say it was a waste of money but my curiosity was piqued and I felt I had a point to prove, not just to those who had finished my career but to myself too.

I had no access to the fire service manuals, being a persona non grata but I did have a number of the old 'Manuals of Firemanship'. some dating back to the 1960s. Scouring the charity shops, I bought a number of GCSE and A level (High School Diploma/ Associate's Degree equivalent) study guides for Maths, Physics and Chemistry for 20p each, running firefighting and hydraulic equations through my head and on paper again and again. Flow Rates, Bernouilli's Theorem, jet reaction; I began to be able to reel them off in my sleep.

Afternoons became a rush to bang out a couple of fruitless job applications and then continue my quest for knowledge like a man possessed; before long we were at the examination date.

Two days of examinations at the West Midlands Fire Service Academy in Smethwick, a three-hour exam, morning and afternoon on a Thursday and Friday. I recognized the invigilator; he was Bill Gough, a West Midlands Fire Service senior operational officer of some note and widely regarded as one of the most experienced and best operational firefighters in the UK; a big player. Friends of mine in the west midlands brigade had referred to him as '*The best Chief we never had*' and '*Billy the Ba*****d*' for his famous fearlessness to call out those who weren't up to scratch, including senior officers. A man who demanded absolute excellence but was universally known as the best in the business. He lived and breathed firefighting and had dedicated his life to making firefighters safer and able to perform more effectively.

I sat down and as the papers were handed out, I seemed to transcend my surroundings, back into the same zen-like state I'd felt at Milling Court. Maybe the countless hours of preparation, time spent whilst others were working, had given me a hunger and some advantage. I just knew all the answers to the questions and seemed to have all the time in the world to express them.

One of the few exceptions I'd made, whilst eBaying what few possessions of worth I had, was the silver fountain pen, given to me by Mr Coles the lawyer: now its ink flowed effortlessly over page after page.

Following the end of the exams on the second day, Bill came up to me; '*Have you eaten Son?*'

'*Not today Sir, why?*'

'*Because I've been walking up and down this hall and the only thing I've heard is your stomach growling. Where are you parked?*'

'I've not got a car Sir, I caught the train, bus and walked'

'Well dive in with me, do you like curry'

'Love it but not had one for a while; money's a bit tight for me at present.'

'Don't be daft. It's on me.'

Bill drove to a curry house near Walsall called the Basmati and bought me a meal. As I tried to scoff it, the rice seemed to swell up in my stomach and I could hardly get anything down. He asked me what was going on and where I was stationed. I told him what had happened to me.

'Well that explains why I didn't recognize you from West Mids. He dropped me off at the train station afterwards as I headed back to Trentside and handed me his business card; *'If you need anything, give me a call.'* With a cheery wave, he drove off in his red Audi. This was a guy who knew the code: a real firefighter's chief.

The weekend came and went: I got through the boxed-up curry in a few sittings and on Monday I was back to the dole office to sign on once again. My job application tally was now well over 800. Glynn smiled his usual smile and said; *'I've never known someone as lucky as you.'*

'Are you taking the piss?' I laughed back and we chorused in unison; *'Yes, more luck than anyone else.... But all bad!'*

As I left the dole office and headed over the road, thinking that I might call into The Leopard, as Paul would usually spot me a pint on the house, a girl ran up to me; *'Can you help? A man's just collapsed!'*

An old boy, living rough, had keeled over on the side of the road. A small crowd had gathered but his scraggly beard, red face and dried vomit on his clothes, meant that nobody wanted to get involved. Knowing my trauma drill, I dropped straight into primary and secondary survey, quickly deducing he was having a cardiac arrest and his heart was in fibrillation.

'Call an Ambulance!' I shouted as I realized he needed CPR.

There are devices called 'Resusci-Aids' which provide a barrier shield for those giving mouth to mouth but most people don't just carry them around: improvising, I grabbed my dole book and punched a hole through the middle, placing it over the man's mouth, moustache and chin. This man had as much right to life as anyone else in that crowd but because of his circumstances, and nobody knowing why or how he'd ended up there, people just stood aside. I may not have been in the job but the heart of the firefighter still beat inside my chest; I began to work.

CPR is hard work; I began to sweat profusely, dripping, as the book began to disintegrate and my lips started touching the old man's. It seemed like an eternity before I heard the sirens but knowing I had to keep working until the ambulance crew could take over, I pushed on. Eventually one of the paramedics arrived and took over, pushing me aside while the other prepared a defibrillator.

The defibrillator reset his heart and the crew got him onto a stretcher and into the ambulance. I never found out whether he lived or died but I had the satisfaction that I'd given my absolute best and done my duty.

As I got up to walk away, a stunning woman with short blonde hair, came over; *'Thank yow for what yow did for thar'old man.'* A full Black Country 'yam yam' accent came out of this petite, beautiful woman.

'It's what I do petal. Who else is going to save the world?'

Chapter 16

Back in the Saddle

I'd taken a chance and given my phone number to the sexy blonde lady and heard no more back but I did get a call from an old friend who I'd not seen for years; '*Ben? It's Charlie. Can you drive a truck?*' In fact, I had passed my HGV license several years before whilst in the Tyne & Wear fire service but I'd been promoted shortly after, so I never really drove for any length of time.

But - opportunity was knocking; '*Yes mate, why?*' '*My driver's going to be off for some time. So, do you want to work for me?*'

'*OK.*' And how!

I reported for work and quickly found myself driving Burton Rubber's truck all over the Midlands, dropping off rubber parts, seals & gaskets to JCB and picking up raw sheet rubber from India at the airport. Each day, took a firefighting book with me and any time spent waiting to load or unload, I'd test myself, or fill my little book with notes. The long hours were spent to a soundtrack of Radio 2, The disc jockeys, Chris Evans, Ken Bruce and the legendary Popmaster music quiz, Jeremy Vine, Steve Wright and Simon Mayo, were the people I had most conversation with.

'*How the fuck did you get them on?*' Charlie asked, coming out of the factory one day and seeing the heavy rubber rolls loaded up.

'*Lifted them on.*'

'*Bullshit.*'

At 120kg (270lb) these 5' rubber cylinders were awkward, but with a lifetime of lifting people out of fires, I had a technique to front squat and clean these onto the truck bed.

I demonstrated; '*Holy Shit, that's impressive!*'

'*It's simple mate, it's heavy, but I just imagine it's someone needing my help and it's life or death out of a fire.*'

'*It's a shame mate; if my house was on fire, I'd want you coming into get me out!*'

Sadly, that would never happen ever again. Or so I thought at the time.

The phone rang;

'*Hello yow.*' Lindsay, the beautiful blonde angel had called; '*Listen; I've read some stuff about you online and it's not good. But there are two sides to every story; sos do you want to tell me yours?*'

We met up that Saturday at a little café outside Lichfield Cathedral. For the first time in months, I had some money in my pocket: not much but enough to pay my way. We talked for ages; me about my trials and tribulations: her about her failed first marriage, impending divorce and worries for her kids. She made me laugh.

Parting company, I said; '*Let's do this again.*'

'*Yes, definitely.*' She touched my face, the palm of her hand cradling my jaw and cheek; '*You've been hurt but don't let them scars damage your future.*' Very profound: the Black Country beauty, turned philosopher.

The spring turned into summer and I rolled on; delivering rubber, lifting weights, walking Barney and meeting Lindsay whenever I could. One night, after drinks in the Trooper pub, we took a walk in the ruins of the old Roman fort at Wall and in the soft summer air, we became lovers, the moonlight reflecting off our faces, our bodies entwined in the remains of that old garrison. A metaphor perhaps? Love in the ruins; or from the ruins, love? Her beauty, kindness, grace, compassion stood in such contrast to what I had experienced. I adored her unconditionally.

Heading back from Leicester and Nottingham one day, having dropped off at Trelleborg and collected at Tenant I took a short detour and drove through the council estate (US, projects) where my dad had grown up. Where from nothing, he'd dragged himself up out of poverty: I had to follow in his footsteps. As I reflected on this, by the roadside, my phone beeped. Email.

From: the Institution of Fire Engineers.

Subject: Godiva Award

'Dear Mr Walker, we are pleased to inform you that in the examinations held earlier this year, you achieved the highest marks of any candidate worldwide. We would like you to join us at our AGM and International Assembly conference in order to collect the prestigious Godiva Award.

Completely gob-smacked, I realized what this meant. Not only had I passed the exams whilst terminated from the fire service and without any access to the full materials required; I had passed them better than anyone else on the planet: and to collect the award in a location not too far at all from the place that had tried to finish my professional career! You couldn't write this stuff!

Lindsay drove us to the Hotel at Stratford, and in front of a full house, I asked Neil Gibbins, the CEO, if I could say a few words; '*I want to thank the Institution for this award and thank them too, for the bigger part they've played in my recent life. Having been terminated by a small, beleaguered county brigade after glittering service in a large Metropolitan; without the ability to study for this, I don't think I would even be standing here..* A standing ovation followed, Lindsay was in tears: I saw Bill Gough at the back, beaming and a stocky chap next to him.

'Let me introduce you to Chief Bruce Varner, of the IFE USA branch.' Bill said.

'You've had a hell of a ride young man - Bruce chipped in - *You ever worked in the States? I know a guy who runs the biggest firefighter conference on earth: you want to be back in the gang, make an application and I'll see if I can help.'*

With that in mind, later that week, I downloaded the Instructor application form for the Fire Department Instructors' Conference (FDIC) and filled it in.

Back to reality: delivering rubber, walking the dog and making notes on Firefighting books. An unknown number came up on the phone; *'Ben. Davie Kay from IFRA..'* That wonderful Scottish brogue; *'Mate, I really appreciate all the letters you've written for IFRA and the donations you've acquired for us. I know it's short notice - but do you fancy going to Argentina next week on a mission for me?'* After the horrendous events of the last years, the chance for some travel - and to help firefighters - was just what I needed: now, just to ask Charlie for some holiday.

Chapter 17

South America and Back in Training

I stood at the airport and saw two guys walking through in their IFRA uniforms. Mark Bryce, divisional officer with the newly nationalized Scottish Fire & Rescue Service and Jim Dave, station officer with the States of Jersey Fire Service.

The flight to Buenos Aires is a long and painful experience but as we travelled, we got to know each other a bit. Mark was former RAF man; plenty of time on the tools and beginning the transition to senior management levels. Jim was a firebrand, with a master's degree in fire dynamics; a champion of science-based firefighting but constrained by the limitations of a small brigade full of misplaced tradition and prejudice: well, I know something about that.

After a brief stop in Ezezia and two days of travelling, we arrived at Merlo, in the San Luis region of Argentina:

as we pulled into the fire station yard, I could see all these faces looking out of the window.

'Bienvenidos El Capitan - I am Rico, this is Walter the fire Chief and Mathias the deputy Chief. We are most honoured by your visit to help us.

I don't remember much about that first night; having been awake for over sixty hours, I was absolutely shattered. I crawled into bed and slept like a log.

The next day we were taken in Toyota Hilux pick-up trucks, to look at the various fire stations and small fire departments in the region and to make assessments, before distributing the fire kit and equipment which had arrived before us, in containers. We would also schedule training in the disciplines in which it was desperately needed.

Jim, Mark and I quickly split our coverage into various disciplines: Mark covering technical rescues Jim on haz-mats and fires, whilst I would pick up fire science and strategic command.

That moment; in the ad-hoc way we split up our tasks, would change the direction of my life.

As we visited the stations, some were little more than cow-sheds with corrugated iron sheet roofs over four concrete walls. Fire engines were sometimes an old pick-up truck with a water butt and some beaters (broomsticks with sheets of rubber); occasionally, a 'chicote' or shovel would also be present.

I sat with the chiefs of these stations and went through a rudimentary version of what the UK Fire Service calls an IRMP (Integrated Risk Management Plan). A process which looks at the major and most likely risks in an area and designates resources, budgeting and training etc accordingly.

Now risks can be geographical; populated areas with abundant rivers for example, may need more water rescue equipment and training than those completely landlocked. Risks can be process-based too: a chemical manufacturing plant in an area should indicate more training in hazardous materials response for a fire department.

As the days turned into weeks, we began to really make an impact. Equipped with helmets and bunker gear, discarded by the UK fire rescue services and donated by the manufacturer Ballyclare, we began to create a hybrid system; based loosely on the UK but with strategic plans relevant and specific to the region. The daily training began to show rapid improvements in approach, safety and achievement: the crews were now working in unison, under a clear command structure. Fantastic stuff.

It was during these training sessions, that my life would completely alter.

Fire science, fire dynamics and all firefighting, is underpinned by principles of mathematics, engineering and science. Not as romantic perhaps, as the image of heroic firefighters, saving distressed damsels from burning apartments and carrying them down ladders in a negligee (the damsels, not the firefighters!). But this science underpins everything and the more we understand it, the more effective we can be and the better we are able to serve the public.

Working in a less well-resourced nation, we didn't have access to the technology that's usually used in the UK to teach this stuff. I had to teach it in Castellano (a South American version of Spanish), with next to no equipment or information at hand.

I sat down in the fire station, the rotating fan in the ceiling slightly off-centre and whirring noisily: ok, what could I use to demonstrate this stuff? Smoke moves from areas of high pressure to lower pressure, so when people open doors or windows, smoke will (unless wind-impacted) generally move towards them; like letting helium out of a balloon. The pathways that take air towards a fire and smoke away (flowpaths.) can be like a tube.... Ok; toilet roll tube and some talcum powder to show smoke movement with one end open (bi-directional), both ends open (uni-directional) and perforated (multi-directional).

Flammable range and concentrations of gaseous fuels in smoke to air.... Cordial and water in glasses.

And this continued; I used everyday items and broke each concept of the science down into a small demonstration using these. Bullseye!

The enjoyment and realization on the firefighters' faces, showed me that they understood and it was a lot simpler than how we taught it in the UK. I had a light-bulb moment: if I could do this is my non-native tongue and help firefighters, perhaps with no formal education, to understand the science; to be safer themselves and keep their communities safer, I could do this all over the world.

As we sat with a pack of Quilmes Beer and a bottle of Malbec, around a fire at the top of the sierra mountain range separating the San Luis and Cordoba provinces, I looked over the vast planes and a donkey walked up next to me. As I stroked its back and looked at the cross, the story being that the humble donkey carried Jesus Christ, I knew that I also had a heavy cross to bear but like the little donkey, with persistence, love and keeping the firefighters's code of honour, I could make it.

It was a pivotal moment and, returning to the UK, I threw myself into IFRA work and have since been fortunate enough to travel extensively, helping firefighters all over the world: there was always the feeling with me though, that I could still do more.

Chapter 18

Bright Lights, Big City

As I stepped off the plane at Heathrow, the phone went: Bill Gough;

'Would you be prepared to work in London? I've had a word with some contacts around the commissioner and the London fire brigade have recently contracted out their training to a private provider. You wouldn't be back on the tools but working at their training school as an instructor...'

Having had no work for what seemed to be an eternity, I jumped at the chance and headed straight into London: a short interview later for the training company and I was due to begin the following Monday.

Not being able to afford the train fare, I hopped on the 06.41 at Lichfield Trent Valley and managed to bypass the conductor with some fancy footwork. Getting the tube from Euston to Borough, I emerged in SE1 and walked through Mint Street park to emerge directly opposite number 94, Southwark Bridge Road.

Attached to Winchester House, the mansion abode of Sir Eyre Massey-Shaw, the LFB's first Chief, with an 1878 fire station; the place was imposing and epic: the ghosts of James Braidwood, first Chief of the Metropolitan Fire Brigade that predated the LFB, and a number of legendary figures seemed to hang in the air.

Walking through the gates, I was greeted by my new manager Allan Holloway; recently retired from the LFB and back as an instructor; *'We've got a mix of currently serving and retired at the minute - I'll introduce you!'* Dave Wilson a retired ADO, Nobby, Tonia, Tyrone, Matt Swan, Paul, the two Glenns and others; all London firefighters at one stage. The crack was immediately the same as I'd been used to in Tyne & Wear, all taking the mickey and instant banter.

'You may recognize Mick Lewis here, he was on a TV show in the 90s called Gladiators; do you remember it?'

I thought I'd chance my arm at a laugh here and as I shook hands I said; *'Nice to meet you Mick, you must be the toughest man in the LFB.(London Fire Brigade)'*

'Why's that?'

'Because if anyone I knew had worn pink lycra on national TV, twenty years ago or not - I'd still be taking the piss and I've seen nobody do it to you - so you must be nails!'

A brief moment of silence, before the widest and biggest, most incredible grin spread across his face: what a great guy, true gentleman and good fun.

'You're alright you are...Where did you serve?'

'A Metropolitan brigade in the North east..'

'In the Siberian wastelands?'

'Some areas are like that I suppose... I was a Tyne & Wear officer?'

Deliberately mishearing, unable to resist the pun, someone chipped in; *'You're a tiny, queer officer?'* Cue more laughter.

I quickly settled into life in London's training school. An old friend of mine Nick was from South London, and he kindly allowed me to rent his 'Garden Office' which had a bed-settee in it. The banter was the same as other metropolitan areas, with added profanity: I did notice that the Londoners loved to swear/curse.

We would carry out theoretical training at Southwark and use a facility just outside London for the live fire training; 'Chiltern Fire'. Sitting in the officer's seat whilst taking fire appliances up to Chiltern, we'd pass over Westminster Bridge, by Big Ben and the Houses of Parliament, Buckingham

Palace and other landmarks. What an experience; looking at a British institution whilst riding up front of one of the most famous fire departments in the world.

Long days, working hard, playing hard, getting the South London circular train from London Bridge each night, dissecting events with Nick over a couple of beers at the Great North Wood pub next to West Norwood train station: I was back doing what I loved and really felt at home in the big city environment.

One episode epitomized those early days in London. Firefighters will always try and push their luck on a training course and get away with as little as possible or have some fun at the instructor's expense. Now I personally love this; it builds rapport and a comfortable environment. To an outsider though, even outside London, this may look brutal but one exchange typified it.

A crew of firefighters from some of London's tough East End stations were in: following the usual introductions etc, I asked if there were any questions before we began; *'Yeah, what do you know about this stuff? You're from the north - all you lot know about is being poor!'* Although he was actually closer to the truth than he intended, I knew it was said in jest; as was my response; *'Well obviously more than you, or the chairs would be facing that way, so keep your mouth shut, you noisy cunt!'* With all the class laughing, he said; *'Fair play Guv'nor, well said.'*

I never had any issues at all and loved working with the London crews.

Whilst working on a set syllabus, I started throwing in some of the stuff we'd done in Argentina with toilet roll tubes and other things, which many firefighters said afterwards really simplified things and bridged the gap between the theory and the science. The venue, the history, the twenty-minute train ride into London Bridge at 6am whilst the sun came up and the City began to stir. Absolutely loved it.

And then I had an email;

'Dear Mr Walker, your proposal for FDIC has been accepted and we would like you to present at this year's conference in Indianapolis.' Chief Bruce Varner had done me a solid turn: what a guy

As I went to leave the training school that night, I found myself under the arch with Matt Swan;

'What's happening Geezer?' 'Looks like I'm off to America mate!.

Within a matter of months, I'd gone from contemplating suicide, with a rope in my hand; signing-on and losing all hope; to being asked to present a paper at the biggest firefighter conference on the planet.

Chapter 19

Home of the Brave

I sat on the airport bus to downtown Indianapolis and as the city loomed into view, I saw the venue. The Lucas Oil Stadium and International Conference Centre were absolutely huge. How had I got to here? I could hardly believe this was happening.

After a night's sleep in a hotel room that was nicer than my living arrangements over the last few years, I made my way to the conference centre to register. Wandering in the wrong door, I walked into the trade section and what I saw just blew me away. Huge American fire trucks, ladders at full extension, filled the rooms as far as the eye could see. Kit manufacturers, everyone: music blasting AC/DC's '*Thunderstruck*', as the exhibitors continued to set up.

This was a big deal.

I walked into the 'speakers' room and introduced myself to the ladies behind the desk: Ginger, Diane and Mary-Beth. '*Chief Halton would like to see you; oh and here he is.*'

Bobby Halton strode into the room: tall, lean and granite jawed, with perfectly trimmed short white hair, he looked like Action Man's dad (G.I. Joe for our American readers). Grasping my hand firmly, his magnificent teeth gleaming a warm smile, he said to me; '*Let me buy you a coffee. I'd like a chat*' Sitting with our coffees, he thanked me for coming over: I was a bit embarrassed, I mean; I was a guest in their backyard really.

'*Bruce mentioned that you've had a bit of a tough time.*'

'*Yes, I have really but things seem to be looking up*'

'*Tell me about it.*'

So I let rip. For about forty-five minutes, I told Bobby all the stuff that you've read so far in this book: at times, this great statesman and ambassador looked horrified and aghast but also I think, approving of my endurance.

'*You're in the home of the brave now son. And by God, you've got bravery in spades.*'

'*It's how I try and live Chief. By the four petals of the Maltese Cross, symbol of the firefighter; Bravery, Loyalty, Courage and Compassion.*'

'*Good man!*'

The next day Bobby gave an inspirational opening address, .Duty, Honour, Country; the three tenets that General MacArthur espoused as the qualities that we should live by. As I sat in the audience, I felt deeply at home in that environment of firefighters, brotherhood and vocation: although a stranger in the US, I sort of felt I'd returned home.

Just before my teaching session, Bobby had corralled a larger audience and stepping into the room, he introduced me to all attending; '*Ben Walker is simply the best that the UK Fire Service has to offer. Not only professionally, but personally he has overcome many hurdles. You've seen the film Cinderella Man, well this guy is the real deal...please welcome to the stage...*'

I nailed the presentation, using the methods I'd developed on IFRA missions and the audience lapped it up. As my confidence grew, I began to warm up and even told a few jokes, one stolen from Ricky Gervais; '*I'm from a small place called England. You might have heard of it. We used to run the world before you lot!....*'

I loved it, the audience loved it. And following a standing ovation, a tall mustachioed, spectacle-wearing bear of a man came up and shook my hand; '*Paul Enhelder, Chicago Fire Dept, how do you fancy riding out with us next week?*'

Paul drove me from Indianapolis to his home in Chicago, where he and his wife Sherri kindly took me in for a week. We gatecrashed the Commissioner's Saturday Brunch, where Paul introduced me to the shell-shocked, bathrobe-wearing Jose Santiago, as the Chief of Training for the London Fire Brigade! I didn't correct him; I was riding out with Squad 1 of the Chicago Fire Dept, downtown!

As much as I'd like to be able to tell tales of daring heroics; to be honest, not much really happened. A few standard kitchen fires and such but mainly, I learnt a lot about the approach and ways of working of an historic US fire department. Great people and so welcoming.

And before I knew it, it was time to get back to little old England and that corner of London where we trained those protecting and serving the metropolis.

Chapter 20

Jimmy Braidwood's Tears

'There are some changes happening here.' This from a senior manager of the company running the training school; *'We're leaving Southwark and moving to two new venues at Beckton and Park Royal, with our own new fire training units that we've designed personally. Also, we're bringing in our own teams and most of the LFB secondees are going to be returned to station over the next few months.'*

From a selfish perspective, I loved Southwark but from a practical perspective, my daily commute from Nick's to work would now consist of;

- Walk to West Norwood station
- Train ride to Crystal Palace
- Overground Rail to Canada Water
- Tube to Canning Town
- Docklands Light Rail to Galleon's Reach
- Bus to Galleon's Shopping Centre
- Walk ten minutes to training school.

All in all, about an hour and forty minutes, to cover a distance of eleven miles as the crow flies.

The company bought new guys in who were 'retained' duty firefighters from semi-rural fire departments. They were nice guys and to be fair, they'd passed the same qualifications as you or me. At the time though, they seemed a bit naïve: not bad guys at all, but at that stage they lacked the 'edge' that being in a Metropolitan or urban fire department brings. Less experience, less 'battle hardening' and perhaps a bit 'softer' in approach: they certainly wouldn't be calling people cunts; whether in jest or not!

As the London presence diminished, the newer guys seemed a bit more malleable than the previous team had been. Wearing SCBA in hot fires, whether teaching or not is very onerous and by raising one's core temperature over 39°c it causes cellular division and that myopathy opens the door for cancers. Having the discipline to restrict your own exposure and that of your colleagues is paramount. Some of the newer lads didn't see it that way though, with the result that they were doing more than they should and working themselves into the ground.

As I continued to teach, I found myself relying more and more on my own performance and materials rather than using any set syllabus. I found that London firefighters understood my simple 'party tricks' better than the information as it was originally presented: I decided that I needed to re-write the rulebook.

In my notepad, using Mr Coles' fountain pen, I began to sketch down the framework for my book, which then was provisionally entitled, 'Fire Science Made Simple' which later became; 'Fire Dynamics for firefighters'.

So, let's fast forward to a late January day, at the training company's other centre in North West London. A couple of courses were running and practical exercises had commenced. That morning had apparently seen some disagreement over the allocation of SCBA wearing, with reservations being expressed about the frequency and potential consequences. I had been teaching in the classroom and was not privy to this.

Dave Wilson had retired from the London Fire Brigade and returned to work at the training school to pass on his experience and skills. He had worked for three departments before returning to London and becoming an assistant divisional officer for a while, in the busy Hammersmith district. Having been an instructor at several locations, he was very wise and very savvy: he knew the firefighting business inside out.

I'd been burning earlier that morning and, with my notebook in my pocket, was heading over to the janitor's room for a cup of tea and a few moment's quiet reflection, possibly making a few notes for my little book. As I scooted behind the back of the 'burn' building. I noticed the smoke. Having attended countless incidents and carried out thousands of training burns, this looked different: the velocity and colouration of the smoke was a lot more lively than it should be. I looked around the corner and saw an unattended Entry Control Board (Monitoring board) and as I approached, I could hear it go into full alarm, with Dave's 'tally' in the board. I looked around and the instructors and firefighting crews attending for training, were sitting doing a debrief some distance away, oblivious.

I grabbed the nearest SCBA set, donned it and fired up: smoke hood and helmet on; gloved up and grabbed the hose. Working alone into the building, I progressed down the stairs, 'pulsing' the flammable gasses in the smoke as I progressed. I located Dave who was prone, half-in and half-out of the burn room. The smoke layer was about three feet off the floor as I lay down and pulsed water into the gasses to reduce the temperature and knock it back. I knew I couldn't just open up the hose and flood the fire as, in that small basement, the steam would push the hot gases down on us causing thermal inversion and 'boil us in the bag' like a Vesta curry.

As I knocked the smoke layer back, I gave the fire a blast and dragged Dave into the stairwell, slamming the separating door. There was just the matter now of getting him out of there: Dave is a solidly built, muscular fourteen stone and 5'11'. As I sat him up, with SCBA and fire-kit, he would weigh in at around 350lb: this would take everything I had.

Every bit of pain I'd been through; all the hatred, all the days locked up; all the days grafting on building sites and lifting rolls of rubber came back to me, along with the words of Billy and Paul, Andy & Paul Insley in the Leopard as well as Shane McQueen and Bill Gough.

'Don't give up, don't give in.'

I had truly been through all of that pain and misery - to come to this moment.

Destiny is a strange thing. Perhaps if it had been someone else, then things might have been different.

I knew if I gave in now, that Dave could die and I would be horrendously burned. As I progressed slowly up the steps, I could feel my lungs ripping out of my chest, my low air warning whistle began to sound: just one more - then another. Finally, I got him to the top of the stairwell and out into fresh air: I ripped my mask off then took Dave's off too, ripping and unzipping his tunic (bunker gear). By this time, the other instructors and trainee crews had realized something was up; one of the operational firefighters started giving first aid. I collapsed, exhausted - and watched. Dave spent that night in hospital and I received a precautionary exam and some minor burns treatment.

'If you hadn't been there, I'd not be here now. I owe you one.'

'It's just what we do Dave. You would do the same for me.'

'I'll recommend you for a bravery medal.'

What happened next shaped my views on a lot of things. The company carried out an accident investigation, I made a statement for this and others made witness statements, yet the outcome was that it placed the blame squarely on Dave's shoulders. No mention was made of the frequency of SCBA wearing and to cap it off, Dave was terminated, under a same ruling as I had been at County; that as a 'contractor', he had no employment rights but would not receive any further work.

The code influenced what I did next: I gave my loyalty to Dave and made the company aware that I disagreed with the outcomes of the investigation and some of the other witness statements. Bravery, Courage, Compassion, Loyalty. Tell the truth, no matter the personal cost.

Suddenly it was like hitting a rewind button. The newspaper article slaughtering me re-appeared and some of the newer guys started gossiping. The 'wife beater' labelling began again. To the credit of the training company; they held a meeting of all staff which I sat in on, stating that nobody was to refer to my spent conviction I was embarrassed at this, in front of all my colleagues but I believe that the manager who did it was right in his intentions, if not the execution.

When crews attending training started asking for me personally, as word of my 'entertainment whilst learning' approach spread across the brigade, some peoples' jealousy went into overdrive.

The company produced an 'explanation of events' presentation, which was delivered to all staff 'in confidence'.

One colleague who described himself as 'disgusted' at the 'sanitization of events', had discreetly recorded the presentation and passed the information to Dave: as I'd been honest about my thoughts, I was prime suspect.

I knew who it was but I was certainly not going to snitch on anyone, although I knew the person involved. I was called into a senior manager's office and asked to name the leak or face disciplinary charges myself.

'Can I have twenty four hours please to think about this?'

'Yes'

That evening Nick and I discussed my options over a few beers.... If I was dismissed again, I would almost certainly never work in the fire service again: we composed my resignation letter and the next morning, I dropped it on the senior managers' desk and as they read it, I told them.

'I thank you for the opportunity of allowing me to work here, and I have enjoyed every second. Being able to train and serve London's firefighters has been a wonderful privilege: I wish you, them and all, the best wishes for the future but I now feel I would be unable to discharge my duties without compromise given recent events.'

On the way out, a recruit firefighters' training course was concluding. Their lead instructor, who was a friend and didn't know I was leaving for good, asked me;

'Got any words of wisdom for this lot Guv?'

Thinking about it, as they lined up on parade about to start their career, I ordered them to run to the top of the tower. As we stood looking over the vista of the great metropolis of London, I told them this;

'As you work through your careers, you'll see good and bad; you'll see right and wrong. But the most important thing is to

remember who you work for. It's not me, not the Commissioner, not the Brigade but the people! Look out over all the houses, the flats, the buildings from here: they're your bosses. Every man, woman or child who lives in or visits this great city. If you can look in the mirror and say that you haven't failed them, then that's enough. Be careful out there, and most of all...Stay Lucky!'

And as I walked away to get the tube to Euston, London was over. I rode the train back to the Midlands, imagining the ghost of Jimmy Braidwood shedding a tear over this prodigal son, as a solitary tear rolled down my cheek.

Chapter 21

Rebel turns Guru

So; back on Trentside, mowing my dad's tiny bit of lawn; I weighed up my next options.

I made a few calls to UK fire services but to no avail; talking to HR people following a checklist; not their fault. I had a lot to bring to the party but no invitation. I did what I could to make ends meet and to try and provide what semblance of partnership I could for Lindsay.

One of my most shameful regrets in life was that while I was away doing my best for IFRA & London's firefighters and public, Lindsay's mother, was diagnosed with breast cancer which rapidly metastased and took her life. I am so deeply sorry, that I didn't really realize or focus on the seriousness of her condition and its emotional effect on Lindsay. I was there but I know I let her down: I should have done more and it epitomizes my own fallibility and flaws. If she ever reads this, I hope she can understand my remorse and shame, for not giving enough when it was really needed, to the woman who'd taught me to love, to give and to trust again. I won't dwell but it's a burden I bear and unlike my criminal record, one I actually deserve and it weighs me down daily.

So, back to firefighting;

My good friends Dave Payton and Iain Evans at West Midlands fire service invited me down to do some training with them. The guys were running a really good, live fire training program and asked my thoughts. We came to an arrangement where I'd help the team out when they were short on staffing and in return, I could keep my 'competence' in by participating and being assessed as both instructor and participant.

Between burning in the Black Country with Dave and Iain, working for my dad, making ends meet and trying to be there for Lindsay, though perhaps not as well as I could have, I focused on my next project; finishing my book.

The notes I'd taken and observations made over a lifetime and particularly the last few years, were pinned to the wall and I sat down at my makeshift desk in dad's garage and began; one Friday morning. Putting complicated concepts into straightforward terms and using words that anyone can understand, examples that anyone could relate to, regardless of their level of education, I let it all flow in a stream of consciousness. Breaking for a couple of hours sleep here and there, by Sunday night I had a completed draft of a manuscript.

Tidying this up over the next few weeks, I began to send a few emails to people with the education and scientific background to critique it. Jim, my IFRA colleague, with his Masters degree, Doctor Paul Grimwood, ex LFB and author of several books, and Neil Gibbins the Chief Executive of the Institution of Fire Engineers. The feedback was overwhelmingly positive: 'This book could really improve things at a grass roots level for firefighters everywhere'.

Now just to get published.

I sent the manuscript to publishers left, right and centre. Polite 'no thank you' letters were received but I plodded on: until one day I got a call from Andrew Lynch, the editor of FIRE magazine;

'We've read your manuscript and our parent company Pavilion Media would like to publish it.'

Back of the net!

I was introduced via email to Mike Benge, senior editor at Pavilion and we began to correspond. Mike just 'got it'. I maintain to this day that his theoretical knowledge of firefighting is as good as most operational firefighters and he engaged completely in the mission that this book would save lives. He worked ceaselessly; cross referencing the book with Bloom's Taxonomy (a teaching structure) to ensure it was pitched correctly and he deserves a massive amount of credit for the outcome.

In the interim, I'd begun to correspond with a hero of mine, Shan Raffel from Brisbane, Australia. Architect of the 'BE-SAHF' model of 'Reading Fire' for fire commanders; assessing buildings, environment, smoke, air, heat and flame factors. Aussies and Brits are quite similar in outlook and we noted an uncommon synergy; our outlook and values just matched. Now, tying in with Bill Gough (remember him), we developed a triple presentation on Firefighter Safety, Science and Command. We delivered it at FDIC, my second appearance: we seemed to be on top of the world.

But back home, I still couldn't get a job. Delivering top information and entertaining presentations at the biggest show on earth, authoring a bestselling reference book but untouchable in my country.

Ric Jorge, Miami firefighter and US Fire Service sage told me; '*Brother, A man can never be a prophet in his home land.*'

As I sat in contemplation, the phone rang; '*Ben. Bobby Halton; I've been looking at our feedback forms from your class at FDIC and speaking to a few people: everyone has said what a nice guy you are. A friend of mine runs the Honeywell Scholarship program, how would you like to keynote at their dinner?*'

An offer I could not refuse.

I knew I had to get this right as so much was riding on it: I went to see a specialist coach called Priscilla Morris, whom Dr Pickerden, a noted management scholar from Birmingham, recommended, and as I discussed my life and events, I asked her what I could say to inspire the Scholarship recipients to go back and make things better in their fire departments and for their communities; '*Tell them what you just told me!*' Priscilla helped me shape and format a presentation and worked on my delivery, poise and voice rhythm and clarity.

Before long we were ready.

Chapter 22

American Hero

I stood up in front of the Scholarship Recipients and guests in the Crowne Plaza in Indianapolis.

'Ladies, Gentlemen, Scholarship recipients. You are here tonight as you have been recognized for your contribution, potential and ability to improve things. But how do you improve things as everything else falls to pieces around you?

Simply, it's about what you give. What you give to others creates positivity and magnetism and good things will happen.'

I proceeded to tell my story and received a five-minute standing ovation and backslapping all round; some people were in tears. Ironically, the high fives that had presaged my original downfall were received once more.

Shan sat in the audience and beckoned me over; *'We've just been contracted for two more books mate.' 'We better get started then.'*

Those books became 'Reading Fire' and 'Fighting Fire' and have helped firefighters across the globe.

As time has passed, I've came into contact with some great people inside and outside the Fire Services worldwide; some who have also been shamefully treated for challenging the status quo in the name of progress. Their stories resonated with mine and I now consider some of these 'dissidents' to be my dearest friends and closest allies. Martin Arrowsmith, Bill Gough and many, many more; still contributing and still fighting to make things better.

I stayed in America for a while, visiting departments and training schools as a guest lecturer. This was organized by a great guy and well-respected Fire Chief called Dave Casey. Everyone loves the fire science party tricks and hopefully at three am, some people will remember that the flowpath is that toilet roll tube and not to get on the wrong side of it!

Shan and I developed an online group to provide technical training to firefighters in the third world, which has developed into an online certification program; with many of these guys going onto pass IFE exams, as we had done before.

Although I haven't much money, I can stand up and say that, despite my adventures;

'I have contributed.'

And far from the end; I'm only getting started.

Chapter 23

The Next Episode

So where did we go from there? I spoke to Butler only last week and he told me that I reminded him of the 80s TV show 'A-Team'; paraphrasing, he riffed; '*In 2010, A decorated firefighting officer was sent to jail for a crime he didn't commit. Escaping via the London underground, he survives as a firefighter of fortune, training services all over the planet. If your fire department is in trouble and nobody else can help - if you can find him: maybe you can hire... The Fireman!*'

And really, he's right. Although my demise and fall was extremely unpleasant and there were times when I thought all hope was gone; not many people are pushed to their absolute limits and remain unbroken.

Now, I know I'm flawed and very damaged in some ways: but I've proved that I can endure for the benefit of others. And living, truly is about the giving. Giving to others and living by the code of the firefighter. I truly believe that if I hadn't tried to give something to others when I had nothing myself and things were getting worse every day, then I wouldn't be here writing this. If I had just been selfish or self-absorbed, then I would be in the grave.

We can all live with honour, no matter our circumstances. It's why I despair when I look at certain developments at high levels in the UK fire industry; people getting rich at the expense of those we protect and serve.

Not for me.

Not my kind of men and women, whether they hold honours or not.

I've been blessed that through all of this, my dad and my dear true friends old and new, have stood by me: people have come into my life at the right time, for the right reasons.

I don't know if there's a heaven but if there is, good guys are looking down on me. It's not my time to ride God's Fire Truck quite yet, but it's in capable hands. Plus, when I do arrive, God'll have to give up his favourite armchair anyway!

Sadly, Barney passed away at the age of twelve and a half. He'd kept me going and lived a long, wonderful life. He was my best friend and loved like no other: truly a million-dollar dog! Lindsay and I parted eventually; our respective paths in life starting to diverge but I will never forget the love she gave me and I cherish her dearly: she will always remain part of me and I truly wish her only the greatest chances in life, she will always be a part of me and her kindness, beauty and compassion will forever run through my heart and veins.

So, here I am again sitting in The Leopard; with Paul, Andy, Rob and a couple of the boys.

And there's another phone call; '*Are you the guy they call El Capitan?*' The accent is East Coast USA; '*Can you help us with something?*'

So, as this chapter closes, I'm just off the plane, into the arrivals lounge in a major American city. Collecting my bag and walking through arrivals, I hear a loud whistle and turning towards it, I see the white helmet being tossed towards me.

Reaching out with one arm, I catch it with a firm grip and hold fast.

THE END...

Or is it?

Ben Walker will return in
'The further adventures of The Fireman..."

.

POSTSCRIPT

Many of you may ask, and rightfully so, 'Did all this really happen?' While others may cast a cynical eye over this story: well dear reader, opinions are like assholes; everyone has one! I may not agree with it but remember that many have died for your right to express it.

I will tell you that some characters have been merged into and some incidents have been combined for the purposes of storytelling; there are also occasional distortions to timelines.

Some names have been changed of people who preferred not to be mentioned and others have been changed to protect them from any backlash. They might have treated me dreadfully but they still deserve the opportunity to redeem themselves; it's not for me to force that situation.

But....

There are enough people around, mentioned within; who can verify certain real events this story is based on...

Feel free to discuss but learn from my story; don't make the same mistakes and above all; uphold the code of the firefighter

Ben Walker
February 2018

Appendix 1

Letter from Danielle Jackson to Tyne & Wear Fire Service

Date: 11 May 2011
Ref: DJ/LC/01W18676/3
From: Danielle Jackson- Solicitor
To: Linda Lauren- Brigade Welfare officer:
RE: BENJAMIN ASHLEY WALKER

Dear Ms Lauren,

We write further to you in addition to our meeting with you at Newcastle magistrates' Court when the above was due to stand trial in respect of allegations of common assault upon his estranged wife Tamara Walker.

To give you a complete picture of events in this case, we first represented Mr Walker following his arrest of the 6th October 2010 when he requested the services of a duty solicitor.

Mr Walker had been arrested at 13:44 hrs at his home address on that day and we attended the police station at 20:00hrs to be present during an interview.

It was clear from Mr Walker's instructions at the time that he was denying any assault upon Tamara Walker and he denied any assault during the interview. The police did have a statement from Tamara Walker that suggested that she would not support a formal prosecution against Mr Walker.

As a consequence of this interview Mr Walker was informed that no further action was to be taken with regard to this matter, however the police then indicated that they wished to charge Mr Walker with an allegation of Breach of the Peace and place him before magistrates on 7th October 2010, but again, following representations by us, that charge was then dismissed and the police then indicated their indication to arrest Mr Walker for Threats to Kill, which they did, and on 7th October, again we attended the police station. At no time were we given any information that supported any allegation of threats to kill, and following further representations being made to the custody Sergeant, Mr Walker was released and advised that no further action was being taken in that matter and he was not interviewed as no complaint had been made.

On reflection, bearing in mind how this case has eventually concluded, it may be that the police were always wanting to secure some kind of conviction against Mr Walker, bearing in mind the lengths they went to on 6th October to achieve the same, and without the assistance of legal representation, they may have actually achieved their aim at the time.

It was certainly put to Mr Walker during the interview of 6th October 2010 that an officer had seen Tamara Walker cowering against a wall, with a male, she knows to be Benjamin Walker standing over her. The officer suggests he was aggressive in his stance, to which upon seeing the police he took a step back and looked to calm down.

Again, following intervention by the legal representative in this interview, regarding the officer's ability to see through solid wooden doors, a further statement was made by this officer, who gave evidence at the trial, clarifying that she could NOT see who opened the front door and it WAS a solid wooden door that she COULD NOT SEE THROUGH, but as it was opened, Tamara Walker was to the left of her against the wall, with her back to her, cowering down and Benjamin Walker was standing over to the right of her.

The recordings of this interview were not provided by Northumbria police despite many requests under disclosure protocols, and in the trial this officer reverted to the original claim that she was able to see Mr Walker whilst approaching the property, which was retracted during the interview.

As was outlined in the trial, Tamara Walker had taken upon herself to have a document drafted which we suggested was an anti-adultery agreement, yet she suggested was a document to prevent bad behaviour, but essentially this took away Mr Walker's rights within the matrimonial home and at the present time Mr Walker has equity within said home of over £100,000.

Mr Walker, following his arrest on the 6th October and his many, many, hours in custody, sought advice from our family law department, and it was following a letter sent (by our family department), challenging the legality of the document drafted by Tamara Walker, which in our view resulted in the further (historic) accusations being made on 20th October, our letter being sent on the 13th or 14th October. ***sufficient time in an interim period to concoct stories and alibis***

The police contacted Mr Walker and indicated that they wished to speak to him further and Mr Walker tried his utmost to have the matter dealt with as soon as he realised that the police were wishing to speak with him and in fact went to the police station insisting that they dealt with the allegation, but they would not do so, clearly at the behest of DC Darkman who clearly oversaw these matters.

On the 4th November, Mr Walker voluntarily attended Etal Lane police station where he was arrested for offences of assault. We challenged the legality of that arrest, quoting law that suggested an arrest was not necessary, as he was there voluntarily and happy to be interviewed. The police would not de-arrest him at that time but somewhat surprisingly, after the interview, the police bailed Mr Walker to return to the police station later that afternoon, which is unheard of in our opinion for a CPS decision to be made.

We believe that the police, realising that there was going to be a challenge to the legality of the arrest at that time and necessity for arrest, bailed him as to minimise any potential compensation which may be awarded to Mr Walker if he chose to pursue proceedings against Northumbria police for wrongful arrest. Upon return to the police station he was charges with offences and due to some difficulties with his mental state, he was detained for court when he appeared in custody on 5th November.

You are , no doubt, aware that a trial was fixed for January, but due to documentation not being available to us (****not provided under disclosure protocols by the police***) that trial had to be vacated, the trial length changed and was rescheduled for 7th and 8th April 2011

You are aware that in the intervening period, there were allegations of Mr Walker breaching bail conditions, by allegedly contacting his estranged wife. It is clear that she was setting up Mr Walker as she alleged that he had entered the house over 12 times, without her informing the police that he was breaching his bail, especially when she then alleged that on these occasions he was further assaulting her!

Mr Walker was arrested at his workplace, (The Tyne and Wear Fire Service), and on querying why that had taken place when he was clearly available over the weekend, the complaint having been made on the 18th of March, the police responded that he had been circulated as .Wanted. but simply could not be found, which in our view is simply ridiculous, and the arrest on the Monday Morning at his place of employment was created to cause him the maximum possible amount of embarrassment , probably again at the behest of DC Darkman who was in the custody area when we attended to deal with this matter following his arrest.

Of course, Mr Walker was remanded in custody at Her Majesty's Prison, Durham before being released on bail by a Judge in Chambers on very severe bail conditions.

Turning now to the matter of the trial;

We had instructed very experienced Counsel in this case, and the writer has watched many, many trials over the years and watched witnesses giving evidence. She also considers herself to be a very good judge of character and able to assess when people are lying.

The writer's opinion of Tamara Walker's evidence is that she was not a credible witness, the writer is astounded that the magistrates', after 5 hours, concluded that they believed Mrs Walker's account which included .independent evidence. and did not believe Mr Walker's account.

It is fair to say that the evidence provided by Davis Peters may have been sufficient to convince of one of the alleged assaults, in relation to the two other allegations, we just do not see how the magistrates' concluded what they did.

You may be aware that the burden of proof lies with the prosecution to prove a case beyond a point of reasonable doubt, and if the magistrates had any doubt, Mr Walker should have had the benefit of that doubt, so for example, if they were not happy with what Tamara said in evidence, but similarly were not happy with Benjamin's evidence, then Mr Walker should have had the benefit of that doubt.

You will also recall that we proved, under oath, that Tamara Walker lied to the police about being pregnant , which should have affected her credibility (***as a witness or person of good character***) but notwithstanding a proven lie (***perjury***) magistrates still indicated that they believed her account!

The writer's view, also on the fact of Tamara Walker. A victim of domestic violence., remaining at Court to hear the Defence's case, is quite astonishing and the writer believes that this shows that she is not the timid, vulnerable, victim she was wishing to portray to the Court, and furthermore, the writer got the impression that the Lady Magistrate was very concerned at the fact that the .victim. chose to return to court.

You will also recall, that at the end of the trial, which of course did not finish until shortly after 530pmon a Friday evening that Tamara Walker was standing at the entrance/ exit door, when of course there was only one way for Mr Walker to leave the Court building, the writer having to seek the services of the police to escort Mr Walker from the building via the police station side of the building. Again, in the writer's view this was done (by Tamara Walker) to provoke a reaction from Mr Walker.

Suzanne McCarton, a defence witness, also expressed a view that she was not prepared to leave the court building whilst she (Tamara Walker) was standing there as she felt intimidated by Tamara Walker.

Since that hearing, we have been made aware that Tamara Walker has again complained to the Fire Service, suggesting that the Fire officers who were present throughout the trial have intimidated her and behaved improperly.

You yourself sat through the Court hearing and know that the seats in Court Room 1 are not conducive to sitting for long periods of time, although it is correct that the magistrates did, on occasion, ask people to sit still, this was not due to bad behaviour, as Tamara Walker is suggesting, but merely due to the uncomfortable seating.

Furthermore, for her to suggest that the attending Fire Service officers who were present acted in any intimidating way is another example of her attempts to wield power in this case, because in the writer's opinion, the officers of the Tyne & Wear Fire Brigade, who were present at all times, conducted themselves in a very professional way. In no time did they act in any other way as, in reality, the writer would have challenged them herself and asked them to leave the Courtroom on the basis that they would not have been doing Mr Walker's case any good.

We then had the final hearing (sentencing) on the 3rd of May, when not surprisingly, Tamara Walker again returned to court. You may have heard discussions between the writer and the prosecutor about the case, and the fact that in the writer's opinion, Tamara Walker is not a victim at all, but a manipulative, deceitful female who is out to get exactly what she can from this situation.

In the writer's opinion, victims of domestic violence, and we see many, as usually by the time court proceedings are instituted, parties are reconciled and the .victim. turns up to Court to indicate that she does not want the matter to proceed. The behaviour of Tamara Walker did not resemble that of any domestic violence victim, as in our view, a legitimate victim, would have wanted nothing to do with these proceedings and left the court buildings immediately after giving evidence, not to return again. Of course, she has done this, in our opinion to .gloat., knowing that Mr Walker is subject to punishment.

Another problem that we have with this conviction and proceedings is that if the magistrates' believed Tamara Walker, her allegations consisting of Mr Walker holding a knife to her throat, drill to her stomach, when pregnant (again all proven lies) and putting her hands around her throat.

You may be aware that magistrates are given guidelines for sentencing offenders;

A custody threshold is normally passed when two or more factors indicating .higher culpability. are present, the starting point being a custodial sentence (Prison).

When we look at the factors indicating higher culpability, the factors that are indicated in Mr Walker's alleged behaviour are as follows;

- Use of a weapon to frighten or harm a victim
- Head-butting, kicking, biting or attempted strangulation
- Abuse of a position of trust (a domestic environment)

Factors indicating a greater degree of harm are also;

- Additional degradation of victim (Spouse)
- Previous Violence or threats to same victim

Therefore, when it is assessed where (if believing Tamara Walker's account) the magistrates should have indicated the sentencing band, this was firmly in the Custodial Sentence bracket. Yet the magistrates banded this in the medium tier of the community band (significantly below custodial).

This seems incredulous for it to be bracketed in such a low band when the magistrates' apparently indicate that they believed Tamara Walker and her witnesses.

The writer can also advise you that this case has clearly been talked about within the clerks at Newcastle magistrates' as when the writer left court on 3rd May, to go to another court and was discussing the matter with a Prosecutor, a Clerk, who was not the Clerk who had heard the trial of 7th & 8th April, made some comments about the evidence, which clearly suggest the matter has been discussed.

The writer is also of the opinion that the Clerk who dealt with the original case is astounded that convictions flowed from this hearing and of course, Mr Walker does have the option to appeal this conviction. However, we feel that, Tamara Walker, having heard the defence evidence, and having been challenged about various matters would firstly, not only lie in any retrial, but further make herself more convincing when giving evidence. ***(This could be costly circa £25K)***

We believe that all parties, who heard this case, save the magistrates, were of the view that this case was not going to be found proved, hence the devastation that following from the conclusion of guilt of the allegations.

Clearly the purpose of this letter is to set out the views of the writer and assist the Tyne & Wear Fire Service in any decision as to Mr Walker's suitability to continue his duties as a serving Fire officer.

Yours Sincerely,
Danielle Jackson.

We do not accept service of documents by e-mail

Ms
Welfare Officer
Tyne & Wear Fire Brigade

DJ/LC/01W18676/3

By e-mail

9 May 2011

Dear Ms

Re: Benjamin Ashley Walker – Newcastle Magistrates Court
7 and 8 April and 3 May 2011

We write further to our meeting with you at Newcastle Magistrates Court on 7 April 2011 when the above named was due to stand trial in respect of 3 allegations of common assault upon his estranged wife, Walker.

To give you a complete picture of all events in this case, we can advise that we first represented Mr Walker upon his arrest on 6 October 2010 when he requested the services of a duty solicitor.

Mr Walker had been arrested at 13.44 at his home address on that day and we attended the police station at 20.00 hours to be present during an interview.

It was clear from Mr Walker's instructions at that time that he was denying any assault upon Walker and he denied the assault in the interview. The police did have a statement from Walker which indicated that she was not prepared to make a formal complaint against Mr Walker and she would not support a prosecution.

As a consequence of that, at the conclusion of the interview, Mr Walker was advised that no further action was to be taken with regards to that matter, however, the police then indicated that they intended to charge Mr Walker with an allegation of breach of the peace and place him before the Magistrates on 7 October 2010, but again, following further representations made by us, that charge was then dismissed and the police then indicated their intention to arrest Mr Walker for threats to kill, which they did, and on 7 October, again, we attended the police station. At no time were we given any information which supported an allegation of threats to kill and following further legal representations being made to the custody sergeant, Mr Walker was released, being advised that no further was action to be taken in respect of that matter and he was not interviewed as no complaint had been made.

On reflection, bearing in mind how this case has eventually concluded, it may be that the police were always wanting to secure some kind of conviction against Mr Walker, bearing in mind the lengths they went to on 6 October to try to secure the same and without the assistance of legal representation, they may have actually achieved their aim at that time.

It was certainly being put to Mr Walker in the police interview on 6 October that an officer had seen Mrs Walker cowering against a wall with a male; she knows to be Benjamin Walker,

7

standing over her. She suggests he was aggressive in his stance, to which upon seeing the police he took a step back and looked to calm down.

Again, following intervention by the legal representative in the interview regarding the officer's ability to see through wooden doors, a further statement was made by the police officer, who did give evidence at the trial, this was PC [redacted], where she clarified that she was not able to say who opened the front door and it was a solid wooden door that she couldn't see through, but as it was opened, [redacted] Walker was to the left of her, against the wall with her back towards her, cowering down, but Benjamin Walker was standing facing her just to the right of [redacted], standing over her.

As was outlined in the trial, Mrs Walker had taken it upon herself to have drafted a document, which we would have suggested was an anti adultery agreement; she of course in the trial suggested it was a bad behaviour document to prevent his bad behaviour, but essentially this took away Mr Walker's rights within the matrimonial home and at this time Mr Walker has equity in that property which probably exceeds £100,000.

Mr Walker, following his arrest on 6 October and spell in custody for many, many hours, sought legal advice from our family department and it was following a letter being sent to Mrs Walker challenging the legality of the deed that in our view, resulted in her making further accusations, her statement being made on 20 October and our letter being sent to her on or about 13 or 14 October.

The police contacted Mr Walker indicating they wished to speak to him further and Mr Walker tried his utmost to have the matter dealt with as soon as he realised the police were wishing to speak to him and in fact went to the police station insisting that they dealt with the allegation, but they would not do so, no doubt at the behest of DC [redacted], who clearly oversaw these matters.

On 4 November Mr Walker attended voluntarily at Etal Lane, where he was arrested for offences of assault. We challenged the legality of that arrest, quoting law that suggested an arrest was not necessary as he was there voluntarily and was happy to be interviewed, The police would not agree to de-arrest him at that time but somewhat surprisingly, after the interview, the police bailed Mr Walker to return to the police station later that afternoon, which in our view is unheard of, for a CPS decision to be made.

We believe that the police, realising that there was going to be a challenge to the question of the legality of the arrest at that time and necessity for arrest, bailed him so as to minimise any potential compensation which may be awarded to Mr Walker if he sought to pursue proceedings against Northumbria Police for wrongful arrest. Upon his return to answer bail, he was charged with all of the offences and due to some difficulties regarding his mental state; he was detained for Court when he appeared in custody on 5 November.

You are no doubt aware that a trial date was fixed for January, but due to documentation not being available to us, that trial had to be vacated, the trial length changed and it was re-fixed to commence on 7 and 8 April.

7

We do not accept service of documents by e-mail

You are aware in the intervening period there was a suggestion of Mr Walker breaching his bail by contacting ██████ Walker and again, in our view, it is clear that ██████ Walker was setting up Mr Walker as a victim of domestic violence would not have permitted Mr Walker to enter the property on no less than 12 occasions, without informing the police that he was in breach of his bail and especially when she further suggested that during some of those occasions he had further assaulted her.

Mr Walker was arrested at his work place and on querying why that had taken place when he was clearly available over the weekend; the complaint had been made on 18 March. the police response was that he had been circulated as wanted but had not been able to be found, which in our view was simply ridiculous, and the arrest on the Monday morning at Mr Walker's place of employment was undertaken to cause him the maximum amount of embarrassment that could possibly have been created for him and probably again at the behest of DC ███ who was in the custody area when we attended to deal with this matter following his arrest.

Of course Mr Walker was remanded in custody following the breach of the bail being proved, for two nights, but was then released on bail by a Judge in Chambers, with stringent conditions.

Turning now to the trial of this matter.

We had instructed very experienced Counsel in this case and the writer has watched many, many trials over the years and seen many witnesses giving their evidence. She also considers herself to be a very good judge of character and able to assess when people are lying.

The writer's opinion of ██████ Walker's evidence is that she was not a credible witness, the writer is astounded that the Magistrates, after 5 hours, concluded that they believed Mrs Walker's account which was supported by "independent evidence" and did not believe Mr Walker's account.

It is fair to say that the evidence which came from ████████████, which of course you will have heard yourself, could have been sufficient to convict Mr Walker of one of the assaults, but in relation to the two other offences, in our view we just do not see how the Magistrates had concluded what they did.

You may be aware that the burden of proof lies with the prosecution to prove the case beyond reasonable doubt and if the Magistrates have any doubt, Mr Walker should have the benefit of that doubt, so for example, had it been the case that they were not happy with what Amanda said in evidence but similarly were not happy with what Ben Walker said, there was doubt, then Mr Walker should have had the benefit of that doubt.

You will also recall that we actually proved that ██████ Walker had lied to the police about her being pregnant which must have gone to her credibility but notwithstanding a proven lie, the Magistrates still suggested they believed her account.

The writer's view also on the fact of ██████ Walker, "a victim of domestic violence", remaining at Court to hear the defence case, is quite astonishing and the writer believes that this shows that this lady is not the timid vulnerable victim she was wishing to portray to the Court, and

7

furthermore the writer got the impression that the lady Magistrate was also very concerned at the fact that this "victim" chose to return to Court.

You will also recall, at the end of the trial, which of course did not finish until shortly after 5.30 p.m. on a Friday evening, that [redacted] Walker was standing at the exit/entrance door, when of course there was only one way for Mr Walker to leave the Court building and the writer had to go to the police station to seek the services of the police for Mr Walker to leave the Court building, again, in the writer's view, this was done to cause a reaction from Mr Walker.

Suzanne McCarton who was called on behalf of the defence, also expressed a view to the writer that she was not prepared to leave the Court building whilst she was standing there as she felt intimidated by [redacted] Walker.

Since that hearing, we are aware from Mr Walker that [redacted] Walker has written to the Fire Service, suggesting that the fire officers who were present throughout the trial, have intimidated her and behaved improperly.

You yourself sat through the Court hearing and you know that the chairs in Court Room 1 are not conducive to sitting for long periods of time and although it is right to say that the Magistrates did, on occasion, have to ask people to sit still, this was not due to bad behaviour, as Mrs Walker would like to seem to suggest, but purely because of the uncomfortable seating.

Furthermore, for her to suggest that Fire Officers who were present were acting in an intimidating way, is again, another example of her wanting to wield power in this case, because in the writer's opinion, the officers who were present at all times, conducted themselves in a very professional way as officers of the Tyne & Wear Fire Brigade, and at no time did the writer see any bad behaviour displayed by any of those officers because in reality, if that had of been the case, the writer would have challenged those officers and would have asked them herself to leave the Court room on the basis that they would not have been doing Mr Walker's case any good at all.

We then had the final hearing on 3 May, when again, not surprisingly, Mrs Walker returned to Court. You may have heard discussions between the writer and the prosecutor about the case and the fact that in the writer's opinion, Mrs Walker is not a victim at all, but is a manipulative, deceitful female who is out to get exactly what she can get from this situation.

In the writer's opinion, victims of domestic violence, and we see many, as usually by the time court proceedings are instituted, parties are reconciled and the "victim" turns up at Court to indicate she doesn't wish the matter to proceed any further. The behaviour of [redacted] Walker did not portray that of a domestic violence victim, as in our view, a real victim would have wanted nothing to do with these proceedings once she had given her evidence and she would have left the Court building not to return again, which of course she has not done and in our view she has returned to gloat, knowing that Mr Walker has to be punished, and no doubt in view of what sentence was imposed, she is annoyed that no restraining order was made, the Magistrates of course indicating that it was not needed.

Another problem we have with regards to this conviction and the subsequent sentence, is that if the Magistrates believed Amanda Walker, her allegations consisted of Mr Walker holding a

7

We do not accept service of documents by e-mail

knife to her throat, holding a drill to her stomach whilst pregnant, which of course was proved to be a lie, and putting his hands around her throat.

You may be aware that Magistrates are given guidelines with regards to sentencing for offences.

We can tell you that the guidelines for these offences are as follows:

Where it is suggested that there is an assault, but no injury caused, the starting point, based on a first time offender pleading not guilty, is a financial penalty.

A community sentence threshold is normally passed when one aggravating factor indicating higher culpability is present, with the starting point being a community order.

The custody threshold normally is passed where two or more aggravating factors indicating higher culpability are present with the starting point being custody.

When we look at factors indicating higher culpability, we can tell you that things which fall into the suggestion of Mr Walker's behaviour are the following:

a. Use of a weapon to frighten or harm the victim.
b. Head butting, kicking, biting or attempted strangulation.
c. Abuse of a position of trust – this is committed in a domestic context.

Factors indicating greater degree of harm include:
(i) Additional degradation of victim – this was his wife.
(ii) Previous violence or threats to the same victim.

Therefore, when we look at where the Magistrates should have indicated the sentencing band, in our view the behaviour complained of, and apparently believed by the Court, would place this in the custody band, yet the Magistrates banded it in the community band with medium level being the appropriate sentencing band. The community band is split into three levels, low, medium and high.

That in itself, seems incredulous for it to have been banded so low for such serious offending, when they indicate they believe [redacted] Walker and her witnesses.

The writer can also advise you that this case has clearly been talked about within the clerks at Newcastle Magistrates, because after the writer left the Court on 3 May to go to another Court and was discussing the matter with the prosecutor in that Court, the clerk, who was not the clerk who had heard the trial, made some comments about the evidence, which in our view suggests that the matter has been discussed.

The writer is also of the view that the legal clerk who dealt with the case was also astounded that convictions flowed from this hearing, and of course Mr Walker does have the opportunity of appealing the conviction if he so wished, however, we feel that Mrs Walker, having heard Mr Walker giving his evidence, and having been challenged about various matters, would firstly not only lie in any re-trial, but further make herself more convincing when giving her evidence.

We do not accept service of documents by e-mail

We believe that all of the parties, who heard this case, save for the Magistrates of course, were of the view that the Magistrates were not going to find this case proved, hence the devastation that followed from them concluding guilt on all three allegations.

Clearly, the purpose of this letter is to set out the writer's views regarding the situation and hopefully will assist the Tyne & Wear Fire Brigade making an informed decision on Mr Walker's ability to continue as a serving fire officer in due course.

If we can assist in any further way, please do not hesitate to contact the writer.

Yours sincerely

Appendix 2

Interview Notes from Danielle Jackson to Witnesses for Defence

attendance note

Client Name: Benjamin Walker
Matter No: 01W18676/3
Fee Earner: DJ
Date: 1 December 2010
Time Taken:

Attending upon a number of witnesses to discuss what assistance they could give Mr Walker in this trial.

The first person I spoke to was Suzanne McCarton. Her address is 38 Fullerton Place, Deckham, Gateshead. Engaged speaking to this lady for 12 minutes.

She is the ex partner of the defendant Ben Walker. She said she and Ben broke up in the middle of 2009.

She said the reason they had broken up was because Ben was "hard work".

That being said however, the relationship ended in a very amicable way and she said that on occasions she was in contact with Ben and in early January of this year, following the death of a close friend of Bens who looked after his dog, Ben had contacted her to ask whether she could look after the dog at the time he was on nightshift and she had agreed to do that. As a result of this a number of texts had passed backwards and forwards between him and her and the first contact she had with his new partner was when she got a telephone call saying something to the effect of "Is this crazy Sue with the lesbian sister". She told me that she was shocked at this being said to her and the person then went on to say "You've been texting my husband". Suzanne told me that she didn't like the conversation and she also told me that she went on to make some accusations about Suzanne to her boyfriend. She said all of this happened on one Friday night in a pub.

She said over a period of time she then received numerous other texts and phone calls, in particular one was saying that she was causing damage to their family, she didn't want her to have any contact with her family and she'd also said she was pregnant. She said it was quite clear this woman was very hostile towards her and although she didn't think she had the text messages she did agree that she would check.

She said really one of the last contacts that she had with this woman following further abuse and threats and that kind of thing, was that she sent her a text saying "I wish you well and I have deleted Ben's numbers and she won't hear from me again". She went on to say that there was nothing bad or malicious or violent about Ben at all and she was more than happy to come to Court to say that. She said that since she became aware of this alleged incident, she has however received another text from ████ Walker in which she was enquiring as to what her relationship with Ben had been like and in Suzanne's view she was simply fishing for information.

She did say that she would check her phone and see if she had any further information and I indicated that we would let her know whether or not we would want to speak to her further with a view to getting a full statement from her and getting her into Court once we have seen the barrister.

Engaged with her – 12 minutes.

attendance note

I then spoke to David Mc█████ the ex boyfriend of █████ Walker. He is aged 31 and he's a service engineer.

Engaged with him some 20 minutes.

He said that there was no way he would become involved in this matter.

Although he sympathises with the position Ben Walker is in and clearly acknowledges that he could have been in the same position himself he indicated "He is not putting himself in the firing line".

He said that he had received a text from █████ in the past saying that she was thinking of going to the police, he was stalking her, people had witnessed bruises on her body, her family had seen them and don't get in touch again.".

Discussed the relationship he had with █████ and how they met.

He said that they went out for about 18 months. He described her as having a histrionic personality disorder.

He said that he met her via the internet. He said he was on holiday in Greece and he'd borrowed somebody's computer to look at his facebook and there was a request from her to be a friend. He didn't know who she was and he didn't think much more of it at that time but when he returned back to England from his holiday he had a further request and then he'd contacted her to ask who she was and what she wanted as he clearly didn't know her.

He said that she'd gone on to say something that she thought that's what you did no facebook, you just contacted people who you liked the look of and he said that they'd started talking over the internet for a couple of weeks and then they went on a date.

He said in his view she susses people out on the website, assesses their vulnerability and she then goes in for the kill and is both controlling and manipulating.

He said they had had numerous arguments over the period of the time and everything which he is aware has happened to Ben has also happened to him or been requested of him in that she wanted him to have fertility treatment, she wanted him to sell his flat for them to buy a property and she wanted him to have tattoos etc.

He again repeated however, no matter how much I tried to persuade him that he was not becoming involved in this case.

He feels that he has had a lucky escape. He said he did try to warn Mr Walker of her behaviour by sending him the e-mail via the facebook and I discussed whether he still had that on his facebook but he said that he believed that she might in some way have been able to tamper with it. He's not sure how, but her certainly doesn't believe it's there any longer.

I explained that this would cause a problem because we couldn't produce the letter without being able to support it's origin.

█████ attendance note 2

attendance note

In any event, he was not willing to help. He said we could ask him further questions if we wanted to but there way he was going to Court.

I then went on to speak to Paul G■■■■ – Engaged 12 minutes with him.

Whilst speaking to him there was a noise in the background and although it didn't dawn on me immediately, subsequently it did dawn on me that he was probably recording the conversation.

It was a very strange conversation I had with this man. He initially said that he didn't believe that Ben Walker had kicked and punched her and I said there was no suggestion of that and I wasn't sure where he was going with that suggestion and he went on to say something about him twisting her arm and biting her.

I discussed the relationship he had with ■■■■■ Walker. It is clear that Paul G■■■■ was a friend of Ben Walker's. He agreed with that. He said that she had rang him one time and asked him to go up and see him. When he went she said that Ben had done off and she wanted him to pass a message on.

I put it to him what was being said in the precise of events from Mr Walker and he denied any of those things had been said. He went on to suggest that Ben was wanting him to pervert justice and he wasn't prepared to do that and the things that ■■■■■ is meant to have said, in particular that Ben Walker had never laid a finger on her, he said he didn't know she'd said that.

I then suggested to him that in fact there had been an inducement for him to be backing off in this matter. He said that he had received work via ■■■■■ Walker. He said he runs a training company and she had booked him in for 10 days but this was whilst they were together, that she had offered this work.

He said that when they first split up he was more concerned about them getting back together. Somewhat strangely he also suggested that they did socialise together but he went on to say that he had never witnessed anything bad between the parties. He went on to describe Mr Walker as very excitable. He also went on to suggest that Mr Walker had a black belt in judo and also undertook Juditsu and he went on to say that things which ■■■■■ Walker had said, he would suggest came from Juditsu moves.

Throughout this whole conversation my overall view was that Mr G■■■■ had been got at and that no way was he going to assist.

I also attempted to ring ■■■■■ but there was no answer and on Friday 3 December I spoke to ■■■■■, having attempted to contact him on 1 December. He lives at 99 Belford Terrace, North Shields NE30 2DA. He is 31 years of age.

He told me that he used to work with Ben Walker. In fact they started fire training together. He's know him about 8 years and he says he has a heart of gold. He said in his view he couldn't see him using any violence. He said he had found the relationship between ■■■■■ and Ben rather strange. He said he'd been to the house once and she just said hello and then ignored him and went onto her phone. He also said that when they were getting married the talk of the

attendance note

station was that [redacted] would be the best man and he'd indicated he would be happy to do that if he was asked and he wasn't. After the wedding, Steve had mentioned to Ben about who was at the wedding and he said it had only been very close family, only about 4 of them, that was what they wanted.

He described him as being passionate about the fire service and a very good friend. He recounted the incident which Mr Walker alluded to in the precise. Ben had come to borrow a van. He remembers seeing a black car pull up. There was then some struggling going on and he could see the driver throw something which he now knows to be the keys and he saw Ben hopping about and the car then pulled away quickly and sped off. He said that at that time there was a lot of effing and blinding going on and from his memory he'd made reference to the fact they'd only been married a couple of weeks.

He did tell me that he had seen Ben with injuries, in particular black eyes but he believed these were from Rugby.

He was more than happy to come and give evidence if we required him.

I said we would contact him again as soon as I was able.

Engaged discussing all matters generally – 24 minutes.

Appendix 3

Letter to Michael Fabricant MP from Susanne McCarton

FAO : Rt Hon. Michael Fabricant MP

RE: Newcastle Magistrates Court April 7th/8th 2011

Dear Mr Fabricant,

I understand that you are assisting Mr Benjamin Walker with his attempts to clear his name from the convictions arising from the above trial.

I was present in the public gallery following my witness testimony and I can attest to the following facts:

My husband and myself were repeatedly contacted by █████ Walker prior to the trial, and during our conversations and text messages we found her behaviour to be irrational to the point where I logged a complaint of harassment against her with Gateshead police.

I was then contacted by DC ███ regarding my complaint against █████ Walker and informed her that I would assist Mr Walker during the course of these said allegations. During my conversation with DC ███ I felt intimidated, her manner being rather abrupt. I told DC ███ that I intended to be a character witness for Mr Walker and DC ███ informed me that character witnesses were not used in a magistrate's court, during our conversation I felt that DC ███ was trying to deter me from supporting Mr Walker. I informed DC ███ that I would assist and support Mr Walker during the course of his trial if I could.

During conversations and text messages with █████ Walker she stated that at that time she was 12 weeks pregnant with Mr Walkers baby. She repeatedly informed me that Mr Walkers was violent towards her and had been for months. I found █████ Walker to be very volatile during our conversations and her manner and attitude would change depending on the outcome of the conversation. During the trial I was later informed by Mr Walker's solicitor that █████ Walker denied ever having this conversation or even being pregnant.

I was Mr Walkers partner for approximately 4 years and as stated in court at no point in those 4 years did Mr Walker display any violent or threatening behaviour towards myself.

I hereby state that I feel and believe that Mr Walker has suffered a gross miscarriage of justice. With this information I have provided you, with regards to events taking place prior to the trial, I hope that you can develop a deeper understanding of the events that have happened here.

I am aware that Northumbria Police are currently conducting their own Internal Inquiry.

I understand that Mr Walker was financially unable to bring this outcome before an Appellate Court, so any help you can give to resolve this miscarriage would be greatly appreciated. If you would like further information please do not hesitate to contact me.

Signed: ST Garton Name: Mrs S T Garton Address: 38 Fullerton

Appendix 4

Letter Excerpts from Danielle Jackson to Ben Walker re Appeals (full letter available with Audiobook files)

Date: 26 August 2012
Ref: DJ/LC/01
To: Benjamin Walker
From: Danielle Jackson

With regards to the interview recordings of 6th October 2010, you are correct, they were asked for many, many, times and never provided by the police (or/to CPS).

Dear Ben

Further to your e-mail I have now had the opportunity of looking at your file again and would comment to the matters you raise as follows:

With regards to the Magistrates' closing comments, I do not appear to have anything written on the file, but I do recall they were very brief indeed and along the lines of they accepted her account and did not believe you and therefore you were guilty.

What was then apparent was that if they had believed ██████ based on the information she gave to the Court, you are right in suggesting that this would certainly have taken the matter out of the community band range and into custody band range and the Magistrates, then when questioned about the banding by the Clerk, went and indicated community band.

I am unable to verify the dismissal of all persons from the public gallery follow DC ████ testimony as the Magistrates wanted to talk to DC ███ alone.

I would suggest that that would have been very strange thing indeed to do. I am not saying it doesn't happen, but I was not present at all times and I do recall being present during DC Kirk giving her evidence and I do not remember it.

With regards to the interview recordings of 6 October, you are correct, they were asked for on many, many occasions and never provided by the police.

In relation to Mr McN███, clearly you provided me with information which would suggest I was speaking to Mr McN███, but I never met the man in person and I spoke to someone who purported to be Mr McN███. You are correct in suggesting that the person I spoke to clearly did not want to come under the radar of ██████ Walker again.

For your information, I enclose a copy of my file notes of those telephone calls which you can see, I spoke to Susanne McCarton and Paul Gil██ and ████████.

You are correct, your defence was based around a financial incentive as ██████ Walker had at that time in her possession a document that had led her to believe she would obtain a substantial financial settlement, but of course, she did not accept that in her evidence.

As far as I am aware, I do not believe DC ███ was subject to abuse from Fire and Rescue Personnel who attended Court and ██████ Walker was waiting outside to gloat or for an altercation in my opinion, but that is all it is, my opinion.

You will also remember that I went to the police station to request assistance after the verdict came back from the Court.

I can confirm that having dealt with your case finalised the matter on the sentencing hearing, when I attended at another court the Clerk did make some reference to it, but again, it is my opinion. I believe that the Clerks would simply suggest that they were discussing it because of the length of time that it took to deal with the matter.

You are correct in saying our advice to you was not to appeal as we thought it was most unlikely that you would have this sentence overturned.

With regards to contact details for Stephen Davies, who dealt with the matter at the first hearing and in fact subsequent police station attendances, say for the last matter, where I attended personally, I can tell you he is how working for a company ████████

I hope this is of assistance to you.

With regards to any suggestion of me attending to give evidence on your behalf, I do not believe that is something I would be able to do, as in reality a lot of the matters which are raised in the ████████

Yours sincerely

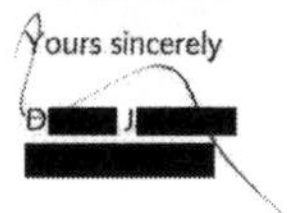

Appendix 5

Screenshots of WhatsApp conversation between Sean .... (Landlord) and Ben Walker regarding illegal surveillance during off-duty periods whilst serving at County Fire Service.

24 refers to a specific station callsign - location of said Fire station

Sean 

Moreton who said he was approached to make a statement about me to help build a case to dismiss me. Just got me thinking is all.

I can't do anything about it now, just my own peace of mind, find out what really happened

Nope, hadn't herd a thing, I was used as a go between as you knew, but I'm not bothered anymore. To far gone for me to even remember dude. Think you should move on for your on health

Sean 

Can't remember the go between stuff? Remind me?

Mate I cant be bothered sorry, just wanted to know what you'd said behind closed doors etc. Told then nothing untowards

Was that [redacted]

I don't know mate, most of 24

Appendix 6

Confirmation of report made to Staffordshire Police by Ben Walker about Tamara Walker threatening/ intimidating him & interfering with other witnesses for the defence:

Cannock Magistrates Court	01543 573164	[illegible]	01782 633105
Stafford Crown Court	01785 211388	S-O-T Magistrates Court	01782 633105
Stoke-on-Trent Crown Court	01782 854080	Newcastle Magistrates Court	

Crown Prosecution Service

The Crown Prosecution Service (CPS) is the Government Department responsible for the review and where appropriate, the prosecution of most criminal cases in England & Wales following investigation by the police. They work closely with the police but are an independent body. If you require any further information about CPS please contact the Communications Officer, CPS Staffordshire Tel: **01785 272200**, CPS Newcastle Tel: **01782 664500**.

Witness Intimidation

It is an offence to do anything intended to harm or intimidate a person who is assisting or has assisted in the investigation of an offence or who is, will be, or has been a witness in criminal proceedings.

If at any stage you are threatened or intimidated by any person in respect of the information you have provided in this statement, or you have any queries concerning the giving of this statement, please contact the officer whose details are given below, or our Witness Care Department, or in cases of emergency do not hesitate to contact your local Police.

Officer in charge of case:

Or Officer taking statement: Pc 5586 Holding
(PRINT RANK, NUMBER AND NAME)

Police Station: ...

Telephone Number: ... Ext.: ...

Incident Number (VDU): ... Crime Number: ...

Incident 692 12/11/10

Victim Support

Victim Support Schemes operate in all parts of Staffordshire. Their volunteers are specially trained to provide free and confidential information and advice. They can also obtain specialist professional help if you need it. **Victim Support will normally send you a letter, telephone you, or arrange a visit from a volunteer within four working days of you reporting the crime.** In most cases such as burglary, assault, robbery, theft (except from and of vehicles), arson, harassment or damage to your home - the police will pass your details to Victim Support within two working days of the crime being reported, unless you ask them not to. In cases involving sexual offences, domestic violence and homicide, your details will only be given to Victim Support if you agree. In such cases individual arrangements will be made. You can also contact Victim Support directly.

Victim Support Contact Numbers:

Victim Support Helpline **0845 3030 9000**

North Staffordshire

Appendix 7

The Journal newspaper report of Milling Court, Gateshead Fire Rescue

SEVEN people, including a child, are lucky to be alive after a dramatic escape from a blaze in a block of flats.

A man was forced to jump from a first-floor window in Milling Court, Teams, Gateshead, and a three-year-old girl was lowered down to him from the same flat.

Firefighters rescued a woman from the same flat in the block of four in the two-storey building, and also two men from another upstairs flat and a woman in a downstairs flat.

And a police officer rescued a woman from another flat on the ground floor.

The fire, which broke out in a communal hallway just before 10pm on Sunday night, is thought to have been started maliciously.

A woman who discovered the fire and raised the alarm was given survival advice from a Tyne and Wear Fire Service operator.

When firefighters arrived smoke was pouring from the windows and the people trapped inside were hanging out their windows gulping in fresh air.

Armed with axes and sledgehammers, the crew smashed their way into the building.

Acting watch manager Benjamin Walker based at Gateshead East fire station said: "We rescued four people and assisted in the rescue of a fifth. All were given oxygen at the scene and several were taken to hospital for checkups, but it doesn't appear that anyone was seriously injured.

"This could have been catastrophic. The fire had been burning in the hallway for some time and had gone undetected because of a lack of fire protection or smoke alarms.

"No one was aware of the fire or was given any warning until the fire started penetrating the four flats."

The cause of the fire is being investigated by the fire and rescue service and the police.

Mr Walker added: "It started in the hallway and we suspect it was malicious ignition."

He praised the teamwork and swift actions of the emergency services, adding: "Their co-ordinated response and professionalism prevented a tragedy from occurring." Lawrence Walden, 69, who lives in the street said: "I was having a smoke at the door when I saw three fire engines and smoke coming from the block. I then saw a man being led to an ambulance. He was limping a bit so he might have been the one who jumped out of the window."

Over the next couple of days Tyne and Wear Fire and Rescue Service will be visiting neighbouring properties in the area to offer them free home safety checks; providing information and advice on how to stay safe from fire and fitting free smoke alarms.

Appendix 7

Report of Benjamin Walker Conviction 2011 - *Newcastle Evening Chronicle*

Gateshead firefighter convicted of assault on wife

FIREMAN Ben Walker subjected his pregnant wife to a campaign of abuse...even holding a power drill to her stomach.

The violent thug punched, kicked, and throttled his new wife within months of them getting married.

And the 31-year-old, respected as a pillar of the community, even turned on a power drill and chillingly pointed it at her stomach.

Newcastle Magistrates' Court heard the abuse only stopped when his wife ████ Walker plucked-up the courage to tell the police and press charges.

Now, Walker, who was living with his wife in Newcastle City Centre but moved down south, has been convicted of two charges of assault by beating and a further charge of common assault.

The former crew manager at Gateshead East Community Fire Station denied any abuse had taken place but was found guilty after trial.

The court heard that the couple married in June last year, five months after they met, and the abuse started just two months into the marriage.

Edith Sanderson, prosecuting, told magistrates both Mrs Walker's mam and a builder had witnessed at least two of the attacks.

One of the worst assaults happened when Mrs Walker was in the dining room of the couple's home.

Ms Sanderson said: "The defendant got hold of her by the head and was applying pressure and squeezing her head and then put his hands around her neck.

"She told him she was pregnant. He then got a drill and put it against her before turning it on. He then pointed the drill towards her stomach."

The court heard that in another incident, the couple were driving when they argued and Walker again turned aggressive. He then lashed out and bit his wife's ear and grabbed her arm while she was driving.

In a victim statement read out to the court, Mrs Walker said she had lived in fear and had gone from being "a happy, confident woman to a nervous wreck".

She said: "Ben emotionally blackmailed me and said that because of his job as a fireman, I would not be believed if I rang the police."

D███ J████, defending Walker, said he still maintained he had never abused his wife and that Mrs Walker was "making-up" the claims for financial gain in the divorce.

Walker was sentenced to a 12-month community order with six months supervision. He was also ordered to carry out 100 hours unpaid work and pay £500 costs.

█████, Area Manager for Human Resources with Tyne and Wear Fire and Rescue Service, said: "We are aware that this has been dealt with by the Magistrates Court and our understanding is that this is a personal matter not related to this individual's service."

Printed in Great Britain
by Amazon